The World where
Sex Was Born

PETER KANTO

The World Where
Sex Was Born

GRAFTON BOOKS

A Division of the Collins Publishing Group

LONDON GLASGOW
TORONTO SYDNEY AUCKLAND

Grafton Books
A Division of the Collins Publishing Group
8 Grafton Street, London W1X 3LA

Published by Grafton Books 1989

First published in Great Britain by
The Olympia Press Ltd 1968

ISBN 0-586-20202-1

Printed and bound in Great Britain by
Collins, Glasgow

Set in Times

1

Lana Lizabeth sighed and the intake of air pushed her mighty boobs out into a prow which would have done credit to an old-fashioned ship of the line.

'Cahm weeze me, darlink,' she purred, waving a hand at Blackie. Lords of Earth had that one arm insured for two-hundred-thousand universal credits. Blackie wondered who had the accent insured, for in early universal language days, a century past, accents had become passé.

Nevertheless, because it was programmed, Blackie decided to 'cahm weeze her'.

The room was something out of an antique Arabian nightmare. Sheer things flapped in the breeze. Huge, padded cushions lay scattered about on the carpeting, which was ankle deep. The room was a riot of color and movement, with cool air waving the sheer things and, by Gawd, a couple of slave girls standing beside an oversized bed waving feather-fans. Blackie sneered. He wondered who the f--- owned the twisted libido that dreamed this one up. He'd had some bad ones in the last six months, sun time, but this one was without a doubt the wildest of all.

Lana Lizabeth was being denuded by the two slave girls. She was dressed in flowing things which molded and ran into the lines of her figure like the draperies on a pre-Christian Greek marble. Her legs were matched pillars of loveliness, exposed now as something long and loose was whisked away by one the semi-nude slave girls. There wasn't a flaw on the sun-bronzed acre or two of skin which was revealed when the girls took away the torso

5

cover and left the idol of millions standing beside a waiting bed in a sexy black pair of panties and a filled-to-bursting black bra which was not hard and padded – as bras were sometimes wont to be – but silken and soft and thin enough to show the taut little nipples perched atop the half-globes of Lana Lizabeth's tremendous tits.

'You would like to feenish the job, no?' She smiled an invitation toward Blackie. The two slave girls were fanning like crazy, as if the lust-object of half the men on Earth were so hot that, unless cooled by fanning, she'd sear the silken pants right off her basket.

'Yeah, sure,' Blackie said, taking a couple of sinking steps across the deep carpeting. Funny how they could do a job like that on something as unimportant as carpeting. He felt as if he were sinking in luxury up to his shanks. Funny, too, how she felt. Her skin was the smoothness of life and her breath, as she turned her face to his and smiled, was sweet and smelling of woman.

'Luf, luf me terrible, darlink,' she whispered, as Blackie pulled a convenient bow-knot at the back of her sculptured shoulders and the silken, thin, scarcely revealing bra dissolved and left the most publicized pair of titties in creation bare to his touch.

Up to that moment, he'd felt nothing. He'd approached the thing with his customary sneer. But the heat of woman flesh under his hands, the very real moan of pleasure which came from the lips of this beautiful, mature woman as his rough, working hands closed over the huge mounds and squeezed – all combined to make things happen. Hell, that's the way it was programmed. He was *supposed* to start panting like a teen-ager and get all sweaty and hot-palmed. He was *supposed* to swarm all over her and savor the body which millions of men would have given an arm or a leg to hold for a minute. Well, hell, he was

6

human. She melted into his embrace and he felt the heat of her boobs on his chest through the thin service blouse.

'But you steel haf your clothing on,' she murmured.

'We can fix that, baby,' Blackie said, suiting actions to words.

Naked and pointed with a weapon which had, at last, been aroused, he grabbed for her and pushed it into the soft, giving warmth of her stomach and she leaned against him and sighed and the results were spectacular, as usual. That woman, he thought, must be ninety-nine and forty-four one-hundredths percent titty. But he wasn't complaining. He pushed and she slid down onto the bed dutifully, letting her legs open slightly to allow his ready body to slip between the thighs which had thrilled a world vicariously many times.

'Now, babee?' she questioned, hoisting her knees slightly in the age-old position of a woman about to get laid.

'Naw,' he said. 'Let's fool around a little.'

'Anytheeng you say, babee,' she whispered.

'Yeah,' he said, 'ain't it the truth?' He pinched a nipple hard and heard her gasp. 'How 'bout that, babee?' he mocked.

'Please,' she said.

He bit her on the side of the breast, leaving cruel, red, indented teeth marks. She cried out and he laughed. 'Hurt, babee?'

'Oh, please,' she moaned, but she was clinging to him with a fierceness which told him, again, that anything he wanted was fine. He picked her up bodily and threw her down onto the bed, her face thrust into a downy pillow. From the rear, she was a thrilling sight. Her rump was unblemished and perfect, rounded and cleft as a rump should be. Her legs fitted closely together in beautiful symmetry. Her back was indented above the swell and fill

7

of her hips to a tiny waist and her shoulders looked as if they had never been marred by the red welt of a bra strap. For a moment, he lost himself in the sheer enthusiasm which the sight of her generated in him. Then, with a muffled curse, he spanked her hard on one soft cheek and she yelped.

But, hell, that wasn't his bag, beating girls.

'Okay, baby,' he said. 'Roll over.'

'Babee?' she asked, face up now, breasts slightly flattened by the position.

'Yeah,' he said. 'Let's get on with it.'

'Oh, babee,' she purred. Her soft, lovely arms reached for him. Her legs opened for him, showing the downy softness there, the love-feathered, inner-heated saddle which awaited him. 'Make eet good for me, huh, babee?' she crooned as he stabbed the waiting lushness.

She was everything a woman should be – soft, hot, moving, clinging, thrusting, fighting; aiding and abetting the oldest indoor game until, with a snort of pure lust, Blackie booted it home in a granglamorous burst of goodness and felt her pulse in reply as she achieved her own bliss. She was and it was everything a woman should be and everything it should be except, Goddamnit, as he lay there with reality, not a Goddamned minute of it was real.

Oh, those motherless bastards, he thought, lying there with the world's most famous and most desired love goddess, the world's highest paid and most worshiped Tri-Vee star still holding him. Those ingenious, bedamned motherless bastards and their little tricks with electric currents and a brain – a man's brain – to be able to put him on a padded table in a steel cubicle and hood a hat of circuitry over his head and make it possible for him, with his mind, to experience any experience he'd ever experienced before with any cast he cared to cast.

8

Those motherless bastards called it the R & R room. Relaxation and Recreation. It was available to the entire crew. But Blackie Decker was the only man to really use it.

The motherless, sadistic bastards. Putting a man on a small ship for periods which extended, sometimes, past months into a year, two years and longer.

He told himself, whoa! He told himself he was a volunteer. He told himself he could be back on atmosphere patrol with weekend liberties in Hong Kong and London. He'd asked for it and he got it, and the service had spent one hell of a lot of money equipping the R & R room with the sensualizer. It wasn't the fault of the service that he used the machine to conjure out orgies with Tri-Vee stars instead of bringing back touching scenes of his childhood or something. But of course the service egg-heads knew that a lowly crewman is going to use the sensualizer for erotic purposes. If they hadn't wanted it used for such sweet dreams they could have wired it to blow a fuse the first time some horny bastard imagined the pants off a girl.

He sat up, all traces of the harem and of Lana Lizabeth gone. Around him was the cold metal of the ship, augmented here and there with utilizable equipment. It was a spartan ship, devoid of the plush fixtures one could find on the big ships of the line. It was a ship stripped to the basics for travel, for she had a long way to go. It was his ship.

He carefully removed the headgear and put it into its place. He swung off the padded table and removed the very real results of his imaginary interlude with Lana Lizabeth from his nude thigh, dressed in simple pull-ons, one piece jump suit and slip-on shoes. He stepped out into the corridor and almost collided with Captain Asa Smith.

9

'Sergeant,' the Captain said, by way of greeting.

'Evening, Cap'n.'

'Bit of R & R?'

'Yessir.' The motherless bastard. Smile, he thought, you prick, you beribboned jerk. Look superior because you don't have to lower yourself to electronic masturbation.

'Well, carry on, Blackie.' That last bit was to show the lowly sergeant that this was, after all, an informal ship.

'Yessir,' Blackie said, swinging off down the corridor. He turned into the armory and made a quick visual check. All well. All was well as expected because the armory was the personal responsibility of Sergeant Blackie Decker, the best Goddamned arms sergeant in the whole friggin' service. Then there was nothing to do. He had a watch at 0800 GMT. That left him plenty of time for a good night's sleep. He started aft; the control door was open and he saw Lt Boots Pastele, slim and trim, slumped down in the watch chair. Before the lieutenant was space.

Gawdamighty it was big out there. Big and black and empty and motionless, although he knew the ship was blasting along still under acceleration from the big proton engines, whose rumble he could feel round the clock in the dayless, nightless, changeless environment of the relatively tiny ship. As always, he was numbed for a moment as he stood there looking over Boots Pastele's shoulder at the viewscreen. It wasn't a direct view of the outside, but reproduced electronically on the screen were distant suns and near blackness and the feeling of the big outside.

'My Gawd,' Blackie Decker said, always and forever impressed, always beguiled by it, by that vast *thing* out there.

Boots Pastele sat up with a jerk. 'Oh, Blackie, I didn't know you were there.'

10

'Just checking, Lieutenant,' he said.

'It's still out there,' Boots said, indicating space.

'I was checking on *you*,' Blackie said, smiling. 'Thought you might need some company on watch.'

'Thank you, Sergeant, but I'll manage.'

'Can't blame a guy for trying,' Blackie said. 'How about you and me having a drink after your watch?'

'I think I'll catch up on some sleep,' Boots Pastele said.

'Kid, you can sleep when you're eighty,' Blackie said. 'Look, give me a break, huh? Knock off the formality. We're on this tub for a helluva long time. Let's be friendly, get to know each other?'

'Sergeant Decker,' the lieutenant said sharply. 'This is a very informal ship. I'm perfectly willing to be friendly with you and with all the rest of the crew. However, some of your suggestions toward what you call friendliness are just a little bit out of line.'

'You heard the lieutenant,' said Space Force Captain Asa Smith, having approached from behind Blackie. 'This is a Space Force ship of the fleet, Sergeant, and Lieutenant Pastele is a qualified, commissioned officer in her complement. I'll thank you, Sergeant, to remember that in future.'

'Oh, balls,' Blackie said, as he slumped his way aft to the bleak bunkroom just forward of the engines. He threw himself onto the bunk and closed his eyes and there before him was Lt Pastele's face, eyes light green, nose trim and neat, a funny, small little mouth and perfect, even teeth. 'Balls, balls, balls,' he said. 'Motherless, sadistic bastards.'

11

2

Captain Asa Smith was quite young to be in command of a ship of the fleet, much less an exploratory ship. Such assignments were usually dealt out to veterans of the service. However, in Asa's case, he'd earned the choice of commands by saving a ship of the line from being pulled into the sun's fierce furnace and by a short history of exceptional accomplishment since his graduation from the Space Academy. He'd shook up the chain of command all the way to the top when he requested that he be named skipper of the *Swinger*, but he'd been promised his choice of commands because the Grand Admiral's son was an ensign on the ship he'd pulled out of the sun's gravity field almost by the strength of his own arms.

Asa Smith's arms were strong, although he was not a big man. He was built compactly and sturdily with a well-shaped head and a strong face. His chin was pointed and his eyes were grey. He visited the electronic barber once each earthweek for a programmed trim which kept his blond hair clipped neatly close to his skull. He was the kind of man people thought about when they thought about the Space Service – tough, handsome, rough and ready and, above all, trained to a degree of competence which, once, men thought impossible.

To become an officer in the Space Service, Asa Smith had undergone every test known to medical and psychological science. So had every other officer in the tiny force aboard the *Swinger*. So, for that matter, had Sergeant Blackie Decker.

But Captain Asa Smith thought that the psych boys had missed a flaw in Sergeant Decker's character.

'Decker bothering you again?' Smith asked his navigation officer, First Lieutenant Boots Pastele.

'Not really.'

'I suppose it is a strain on the sergeant,' the Captain mused, 'being the only enlisted man on board.'

'I suppose,' the lieutenant agreed.

'I believe in running an informal ship,' Smith said, sucking on his lower lip before speaking, choosing his words. 'Yet, I am sure, Lieutenant, that I don't have to remind you of the regulations.'

'Of course not, sir.'

'Who is your relief, Lieutenant?'

'Lieutenant Knight, sir.'

'Carry on.'

In the quietness of his cabin, Capt. Asa Smith made a brief entry in his log to mark the end of yet another uneventful day aboard ship. Six earthmonths and two earthdays out from home, still accelerating. He did some quick and complicated mental calculation and came up with two weeks as the nearest time period, roughly, to their first goal, that goal of reaching a speed so near the speed of light that Einstein's theory of mass and motion was pushed slightly, but not completely, awry.

In his bunkroom, Blackie Decker dozed. In control, Boots Pastele settled down to a routine check of dials and indicating meters and viewscreens, the boredom of the watch having settled over the room again after the interruption by Decker and the Captain. Aft, in a radiation shielded alcove in the forward part of the engine rooms, First Lieutenant John Knight, fiftyish, greying but still slim and handsome, kissed Second Lieutenant Martin.

'Not here, John,' Lieutenant Martin said.

13

'Best place I know,' John Knight whispered. 'Off limits to all personnel.'

'I shouldn't be here,' Martin whispered, but the sound was muffled by John Knight's seeking lips.

In control, Boots Pastele filled in logs. Everything checked. In his quarters, the Captain mused. Six months out, over six months to go. Things going well, except for the apparent deviation from normal behavior which he'd noticed in his arms sergeant. Ship and crew functioning smoothly, building up to jump speed in about two weeks.

Pleased with himself and his command, Asa Smith removed his slip-on boots and propped his feet on his desk. It was a small desk and his knees remained bent, for space, even in Captain's quarters, was limited. He reviewed the situation and the personnel under his command. Blackie Decker, a good man. He could straighten the sergeant out. Have him spend a bit more time in R & R. Some men needed it. Ingenious devils, those scientists who came up with the sensualizer. Early in his career, Asa had tried it. Came on him like a nova, the sensations. So good he wanted to stay in the sensualizer forever. Man could let such pleasures spoil him. But not Asa. He was strong. Man had to discipline himself if he expected to command the respect of those to whom his rank meant discipline. In six months, Captain Asa Smith had been in the R & R room only to make routine inspections, never to sample the debilitating pleasures of the sensualizer. The others made their visits to R & R with the regularity prescribed by the book.

Briefly, Asa Smith allowed himself to be frivolous. He tried to imagine what the members of his crew would turn on when they strapped on the sensualizer. Not hard to guess about John Knight. Knight was a single man by choice, a womanizer by hobby, a good lover by dint of long practice. That the Captain knew. Knight's love of

14

women, any woman within reach, was one reason why he was still a lieutenant at the age of fifty-one. But the Captain didn't condemn Knight. The man was intelligent enough to choose the way he wanted to live and if sex meant more to him than his service career, that was Knight's choice.

But what about the others? Lieutenants Martin and Pastele. What did they conjure up when they were in R & R, with the permissive sensualizer headpiece in place. There, the Captain was at a loss. He did not know Lieutenants Martin and Pastele as well as he knew John Knight. Martin and Pastele had been picked for the mission by computer, had been assigned without question as the way of the service. There had been a time when people like Martin and Pastele were considered inferior beings. Hell, long years ago, they'd been refused such basic things as the vote, the right to live where they chose and associate with whom they chose. They'd been paid less for doing the same jobs, assigned to special units in the various services. That age of discrimination was long past, of course, but people of Martin and Pastele's type were still more alien to Asa Smith than men like John Knight, a career service man from North America.

The Captain quickly gave up the idea of trying to figure what Martin and Pastele would program into the sensualizer. Hell, they were human, and would probably indulge in the same sexual fantasies which the psych boys said were pretty standard among the type of person who was superior enough to make the grade in the service, normal, heterosexual fantasies with, occasionally, normal deviations into orgiastic behavior.

Whatever the two lieutenants did under the sensualizer, it didn't matter to Asa Smith – a man with a will so strong that he would hold his sexual energies inside him until he had returned to Earth, until he was back with his wife,

Elenore. Elenore would be, it being evening, North American time, at home from the office where she worked to kill time while her husband was on fleet service. Perhaps she'd be having her evening meal or taking a bath – sensual pictures flashed into Asa's mind for an unguarded moment, bared, soft woman flesh, long legs, sweet saddle which had known his kisses – or preparing for an evening out with friends. Whatever it was she was doing, he knew that his wife, Elenore Bradly Smith, daughter of Grand Admiral Southworth P. Bradly, Retired, wife of the upcoming Captain Asa Smith, would be doing it with dignity and foresight.

'Are you sure no one will come?' Lieutenant Martin whispered in Lieutenant Knight's ear, as Lieutenant Knight's hands went exploring inside Lieutenant Martin's service jumpsuit.

'Well, maybe a couple of us,' Knight joked rudely, 'but no one will *interrupt*.'

Lieutenant Pastele yawned and made the quarterhour readings. The control room was quiet, even as instruments hummed and moved, showing the life of the ship.

Sergeant Blackie Decker rolled over. He was dreaming that he was eating a non-synthetisized steak in Joe's Bar back on Earth with a slut waiting to be pounced when he was ready.

A few million miles away, Elenore Bradly Smith, daughter of Grand Admiral Southworth P. Bradly, Retired, removed her panties with great dignity. With equally great foresight, she'd taken her pills with regularity since Asa shipped off to go exploring on the *Swinger*. The sailor she'd picked up on the way home from the office stood at the foot of her bed, gawking at her, still unable to believe his luck. He'd been thinking about going into the fleet R & R base in New York for a quickie on the sensualizer and there before him, in the real, raw, blushing flesh, was a matured, yet young and juicy woman with her dress falling to the floor which was carpeted an inch thick. The sailor clutched himself with eagerness and watched, wide-eyed, as Elenore Bradly Smith leaned down with great dignity and removed her panties. She had used a depilatory and was smooth as she thrust her mound toward the gaping sailor.

'Hurry, darling,' she whispered, 'my husband will be home in an hour.' Actually, she knew her husband would not be home in an hour, a day, a month or a year. Her husband was headed out toward Alpha Boötis and accelerating, according to the flight plans, with the big jump days in the future. Her husband would return, if ever – and being a service brat she knew there was a possibility he wouldn't, having seen many good men go off into space to be lost – in something over a year and a half. In the meantime, she was young and lusty.

She saw, when the nervous sailor had removed his uniform, that she had picked well. He was hung, that boy. She positioned herself on the bed, legs opened, waiting. He crawled to her. She giggled, thinking that if it snagged, he might pole-vault right over her. She was not a girl to waste time with the preliminaries. The sailor tried to kiss her breasts. She seized him, used her lips, her mouth forming a sliding tube of joy, to convince him that no further romping was necessary before the main event. She took him, moaning with the goodness, her legs flying up to point toward the ceiling.

A few million miles away, Asa Smith pictured his wife having a sedate dinner, perhaps with her father, a dignified old man, or with a group of service friends who would, at some time during the evening, inquire about him.

'You say your old man is coming home?' the sailor asked Elenore Smith, feeling renewed throbbings. He was

17

looking at her, all woman and relaxed on the pastel sheets. Elenore moved her head with great dignity and saw the signs of rejuvenation.

'Darling,' she said. 'I told you he wouldn't be here for a *whole* hour.' She pushed the sailor onto his back, mounted, let her weight slide her impalingly down on his member. 'We have loads of time,' she whispered, as she began to use him selfishly for her own pleasure, her frenzied movements giving him pleasure in return.

'Oh, John, John, John,' Lieutenant Martin moaned in sheer bliss as Lieutenant John Knight's hand cupped between hot thighs and rubbed.

3

There on the explorer ship *Swinger*, John Knight knew he was courting a court martial when he took Lieutenant Martin into his arms. His companion in sin, although younger in service and in years, also knew that they were breaking more regulations than they could count on two hands using every finger. However, neither of them cared. They were both officers in the Space Service and they had both been cooped up on an explorer vessel for over six months with another half year ahead of them before they could hope to set foot on solid ground again. When they did land, it would be on an alien planet where earthman had never been. Anything could be awaiting. Earthships had flashed out toward the stars for decades now and some returned – most returned – telling stories of wild, empty space and uninhabitable worlds and dark suns and loneliness. Some, however, failed to return and each explorer had this to face. That thought, perhaps, helped influence the two lieutenants. The threat of death has always roused the mating instinct in man. Yet, both Knight and Martin knew they were risking dismissal and disgrace. Both knew that their Captain, Asa Smith, was a book man who would throw said book at them if they were caught.

But Knight's hand was rubbing between Martin's thighs. Knight's lips were pressing against Martin's and Martin's tongue came out to lick Knight's lips sensuously. It had begun six days out from earth and it had continued with ever increasing intensity until it became a blaze of lust which blew up into raging fires each time Knight and

Martin touched. It was inevitable that Knight and Martin should fall, should forget their service responsibilities.

John Knight was a lusty man and Ellie Martin was a sensuous woman. Those two facts overrode all.

It started six days out. Ellie, on watch, doing her duty with complete equality with the men of the ship, her sex having been freed, at last, from all the discriminations against it, felt John's eyes on her.

She knew she was good to look at. Slim, long-waisted, her hips were slightly boyish but still feminine enough to tell a casual observer at twenty paces, even in the one-piece service uniform, that she was girl. She had long, bell-shaped breasts tipped with a petulant pair of little red-brown nipples. Her shoulders were gracefully wide, her arms long, her neck dainty. She had straw-blonde natural hair which she clipped just below her ears and swept forward onto her cheek. She wore service-approved lipstick and eye make-up, although she needed little of either. Her eyes were brown and mischief was in them, even when she was seriously attending her duty. Trained in medicine, she knew her body as only a competent doctor can. As medical and psych officer, she also knew the bodies and minds of the rest of the crew of the *Swinger* better, perhaps, than any single person aboard, including the Captain.

Knowing herself, she recognized the immediate chemical attraction which existed between herself and the engineering officer, John Knight. Knowing the regulations of the service, that strict code of blue-nose prudery which frowned on normal sex between members of the service and excused the abnormal, semi-masturbatory, somehow evil dreams of the sensualizer, she told herself from the first that the attraction would remain only an attraction, would not flare up into the full-sized affair for which her body clamored as she came to know John Knight better.

20

As for John Knight, that worthy officer knew that he was making his last bid to get beyond the rank of lieutenant. He had volunteered for exploratory duty not because he was a dedicated space man, but because he had just passed his fifty-first birthday and was on his last five year enlistment before retirement. A space captain's pay would just barely support him, in retirement, in the style to which he had become accustomed in thirty years of service. A space lieutenant's pay would be just a few credits short each month. He knew that promotion was automatic upon return from a long exploratory mission and this plus balanced out the negatives. On the minus side there was the ever-present chance that the little starship would vanish forever somewhere in the central galaxy. Before boarding the *Swinger*, there had been one more very important negative consideration, a consideration which was overridden immediately when John met Lt Ellie Martin, with her smiling lips and mischief-making eyes and her bell-shaped breasts which she carried unfettered under the one piece service jumpsuit. He felt the chemistry immediately and knew, by her response, that she felt it, too. When he began to make active efforts to seduce a fellow officer in direct defiance of numerous regulations, it was not the first time he'd ignored those particular regulations. Once he'd been stationed on moonpost with a bevy of young female ensigns fresh out of the academy and, Jesus God, it had been such a perpetual orgy that he was almost glad when he was relieved. Those young girls had almost done him in, even though he faithfully took his libido building pills each morning.

So Knight was not getting a cherry as far as he was concerned when he finally cornered Ellie Martin and took advantage of their mutual body chemistry. He was an old hand at finding secluded spots on military installations.

21

He was an old hand at making a woman feel that she was the first and only woman ever to know the *true* joys of sex.

After a few days of fencing around, back there just out of Earth when the engines had been brought up to speed and his work was finished for a while, John knew that the time was ripe. He had been a bit afraid, at first, that Ellie might be the strong-minded type who would hold out for months, using the sensualizer to keep the natural sexual desires from building. However, his built-in sense of *when* told him that he would not be deprived of what he considered one of the necessities of life, after all.

He made his move in the medroom, Ellie's office. He had gone there on the pretext of needing medical assistance. He complained of a pain in his lower abdomen. Ellie, the efficient officer-doctor, told him to slip out of his uniform and take a position on the examination table. He did so. He spread a stiff, white sheet over himself.

'Now,' she said, approaching him, neat in her white one-piece, 'just where is this pain of yours, Lieutenant?'

'Here,' he said, taking her soft hand and pressing it to his heart.

She frowned. 'You said the lower abdomen.'

'And here,' he said, taking her hand, making his move boldly. He pushed it down on a growing thing which gave a quick pulse of eagerness when her hand touched it. He was watching her face closely. She did not change expression, still maintaining her professional frown.

'The sensualizer can take care of that, Lieutenant.' She removed her hand slowly but firmly.

'Baby,' he said, 'that's for the buck privates in the rear ranks. That's for peons. You and me,' he said, reaching up to seize her bell-shaped, slightly elongated breasts, unfettered under her thin, silken one-piece, 'are far too

22

intelligent to stoop to having ourselves stimulated electronically.'

'Get your Goddamned hands off my tits,' Ellie Martin said. 'Or I will crown you with a piss-pot.'

He didn't move his hands. He kneaded the softness under her uniform softly, skillfully, watching her face all the while. 'Baby,' he said, 'you don't want me to take my hands away from them any more than I want to do it.' He smiled. A smiling John Knight was a not unpleasant sight for a nubile young woman like Ellie Martin. At twenty-five, at the peak of her sexual powers, she could sense the competency in the older men. Having done her share of love-play with men of her own age group in school and during her first few months in the service, she was fully aware of the joys she had stored up in her ample body. She was also quite sure that John Knight would be, perhaps, the most skillful releaser of those joys with whom she had ever come into contact.

'Asa Smith would toss us out a porthole just for this,' she said, not bothering to try to remove John's skillfully moving hands from her breasts.

'I believe that door over there locks on the inside,' he told her. 'After all, a doctor must have privacy while examining a patient.'

She moved out from under his hands long enough to lock the door. She thought about dimming the lights, but decided against it. She took two steps back toward the examination table, paused to run the zipper down the one-piece, stepped out of it into near nudity, covered only by a very un-service-like pair of blue panties cut bikini style. The side bands were about one and a half inches wide and were transparent, so thin were they. The little pouchlike area of material which covered her mound and held other secrets was double-sewn and was, thus, opaque. An abundancy of love-hair caused it to round

23

out, as if it contained so much woman it bulged. Her navel, a full four inches above the top of the panties, was an elongated little indentation in the plane of her belly. She had a few freckled areas above her sweet breasts.

When she removed the panties, John saw that she had not yet lost her earthtan. He saw, also, that she had indulged in titty tanning, because the only non-sun areas on her body were under the bit of bikini panties. She turned to toss the panties onto a chair and the whiter areas on her rump made a pale mask across the rounded nates. There was a sweet little crease at the bottom of each globe which made and unmade as she moved.

To an observer, it might have seemed that the two lieutenants approached coition coldly and matter-of-factly.

'This isn't the most comfortable place in the world,' Ellie said, as she neared the examination table. It was at waist height, in the manner of examination tables, and it was narrow.

'We'll manage,' John said. He let her remove the sheet which had become tent-shaped in a specific area.

'Where did you say it hurt?' Ellie asked, with her doctor's frown.

'Ummm,' John said, hoisting his loins to raise the already elevated object of discussion a bit higher.

'I'll make it well,' she said, and, at that point, all semblance of coldness and matter-of-factness went flying out a porthole as she bent over the man on the examination table and applied one of nature's oldest remedies for hurt. 'Kiss to make it well,' she crooned.

'Ggggaaaa,' John moaned, for she was very artful at her particular brand of first aid. 'Ohhhhhh-uhhh!' He hadn't used the sensualizer at all and he had a lot stored up and she was damned good. 'Halt, stop, quit,' he said. 'Gawd-a-mighty!'

'What's the matter, lover?' Ellie whispered, her voice hoarse.

'You're gonna waste me, lady,' he told her. 'C'mere.' He reached for her and pulled her up onto the table atop him. She held herself up, hands on the edge of the table, did a push-up which suspended one bell-like breast in front of his lips and he promptly chewed it tenderly, making the little nipple cringe with joy and expand with pride. Meanwhile she was searching, her knees on either side of John's legs probing around pushing wetness down on him until the exact detonation point was found and an implosion of passion stabbed her vitals as body entered body. After that, time moved on with a series of volcanic movements matched to each other, curve clinging to curve, hardness banging hardness, closing the minute distance between them until, with a gusty moan, Lieutenant Ellie Martin got her rocks off with great gusto and Lieutenant John Knight followed suit with equal enthusiasm.

One day Captain Asa Smith asked, 'Are you having difficulties healthwise, John? You seem to be spending a lot of time in the medroom.'

After that they had to be more careful. Nevertheless, there were ample opportunities. The Captain couldn't watch every area of the ship. There were always little nooks, such as the alcove in the engine rooms, shielded from the big engines and padded by a couple of radiation suits. In that alcove, six earthmonths and two earthdays out, Knight serviced Martin admirably, with all sorts of little variations which they had worked out during six months of steady screwing. Martin moaned with the usual delight. Knight had the usual satisfactory climax. All climaxes were good with Knight, who had made a career of having climaxes in varying intensities with a series of assorted partners ranging down to and including a female

Venusian bushape, who, incidentally, was quite interesting, having a body temperature of one-twenty-five F. so that it was like putting it into a pot of hot, firm, living pudding. But that particular climax, there in the engine room alcove, happened to be climax number eight-seven with Ellie Martin. That was a record for John Knight, who believed in variety. As he finished the job and buttoned up, after cleaning himself on the sleeve of a radiation suit, he wondered why he wasn't able to make headway with the other female officer on the *Swinger*, Lieutenant Boots Pastele of the funny, sweet little kissable mouth and the cool green eyes and the beautiful ash blonde, long hair.

'Double feature today, lover?' Ellie asked, fondling a doughy lack of virility, John's readiness having been made unready in the cauldron of her squirming body.

To a man like John Knight, it was a challenge. He put his mind to it and nothing happened. He did some inspired muff-diving and roused Ellie to heights of desire which caused considerable agitation there in the alcove and nothing happened.

'Oh, honey, now, honey, now, baby,' Ellie was cooing, reaching for him, not wanting to waste it without that hard core of man inside her, wanting to feel full and complete before she released the pent-up energies inside her.

John felt a moment of panic. He'd never before failed a woman. It was a point of pride with him. Usually it was John Knight who smiled smugly as he laid to rest the last iota of sexuality in a woman. Now he was being called upon to perform and he was as limp as last week's noodles. Then, with sudden inspiration, he closed his eyes and pictured Boots Pastele. New and different women always inspired him. He pictured her breasts, somewhat smaller than Ellie's, shaped differently, more round than

26

long. He pictured her long, blonde hair curling down onto her sweet shoulders and her little mouth under that pert nose and those green eyes outlined darkly by long lashes. It worked and he worked and he even managed a creditable finish by pretending it was Boots and not Ellie who was pinioned to the floor by his weight and his member.

Coming out of the engine room area they met Blackie Decker, who glowered at them darkly before nodding and moving on. John frowned. It wasn't the first time the sergeant had been nearby when he was diddling with Ellie. In his concern about the Captain, John had ignored the other two crew members. Boots Pastele tended to her duties of navigation and stayed in her quarters a lot when off duty, but that Goddamned sergeant was always around, sniffing as if he could smell the passion in the air. And Blackie spent a lot of time with the sensualizer, indication of a rather erotic nature, John thought. First thing he knew the bastard might be trying to horn in, and with only two women aboard, John Knight didn't intend sharing them with anyone, much less an enlisted man.

'Good evening, Sergeant,' Ellie said cordially, as Blackie walked past with only a nod. When he was gone she looked at John. 'Do you get the impression that there's something bothering Sergeant Decker?'

'Yeah,' John said, chuckling. 'Same thing that bothers me constantly – lackanookie.'

'You're a crude bastard,' Ellie said, laughing. She looked thoughtfully after the enlisted man until he turned and disappeared down a side corridor to his quarters.

4

Knight relieved Boots at the exact minute of the exact hour, looking trim and neat in a fresh uniform. He was a handsome bastard, Boots thought. Greying hair which merely added to his appeal, thin, active-looking, sharp-eyed, close-shaven and masculine. For a moment, she envied Ellie. She knew Ellie was screwing the engineering officer. Ellie had never said so, but it was written all over the girl. She'd come back to quarters all limp and relaxed, take a shower while almost purring with satisfaction and sleep like a baby. Ellie was negligent, too, about her prescribed sessions in R & R. With true impartiality, the service said, in the little blue book on shipboard conduct, that all personnel should spend a specified time in R & R each week. And Boots knew for a fact that Ellie some-times skipped two weeks running.

Boots, herself, was a good little lieutenant. She went dutifully to R & R each week and dutifully dreamed up a sweet little heterosexual scene during which some almost faceless boy kissed her tenderly, played with her breasts for a measured amount of time as advised in the sex manuals, toyed with her clit for an equally measured amount of time, and then quietly inserted himself and demurely screwed her until she was rewarded by a demure little orgasm which left her slightly weak and slightly ashamed.

Once she tried to cast the sergeant, Blackie Decker, in one of her scenes, but it didn't work out. He tried to take over and she shut him out and went back to her faceless lover. Again, when it hardly seemed worthwhile to conjure up a carnal scene, she thought about the boy who had initiated her into the lusty but frustrating world of sex and that was worse. The sensualizer was, after all, merely an extension of the knowledge in one's memory and the memories she had of that boy were a mixture of pain and pleasure.

Boots was a small girl. She had small bones and small limbs. Her small mouth was one of the more determinate features which made up her looks. And there was something else about her that was small. When she was sixteen and in love for the first time, that part of her had been so small that she considered, for a while after her first silly effort at getting laid, giving up on sex forever.

She'd been going with Tom for almost three months. He owned a new flyer, his father having more money than most, and they spent their dates in exotic places like Capri and Miyazaki and Matamoros. In that three months, Boots decided that she'd like very much to go on living at Tom's level. Money was a wonderful thing. The sheer ability to hop in a flyer at dusk in her home in Paso Robles, California, and be in Hong Kong or Paris, only a couple of hours later represented money, for flyers not only were expensive, they required a permit which didn't come cheap, either. The government limited them severely because the airways of old Earth were so crowded. But money could buy almost all, including a flyer with speeds high enough to put Samoa within reach of an evening's date. When Tom, who was nineteen, told her that she was his girl, the girl he wanted to spend a lot of years with, she smiled with her pretty little mouth and let him tongue her deep for the first time.

Boots was an old-fashioned one. Her father was a Reform minister. The Reformists had revived God, after man killed him in the twentieth century, and in a world where sex was a universal pastime, because birth control was very, very positive and also required, taught chastity. At sixteen, Boots had had male hands in her pants, but never a male member. However, when Tom proposed to her, she said yes to a lot of things. She said yes to tongue kisses and found them to be juicy and fine. She said yes to breast play, put her soft little hands behind Tom's close-cropped head and pressed his sucking mouth deep into sweetly shaped breasts. She said yes to everything and found that oral sex can be wild, wild, wild. She let Tom do it first, on a date in his flyer, parked on hover over the deepest part of the Grand Canyon with the sun going down. When red fingers of fire laced the western sky, she popped her cookies under Tom's hungry mouthings and thought she'd discovered that Santa Claus, like God, was not dead.

She told herself it was all right, because she and Tom were going to be married, and allowed him to introduce his gleaming member into her small, hot, wet, hungry mouth and found that man ain't bad, after all. He gagged her a bit with his eagerness, but all in all it was a pretty sexy experience. Tom knew that he had himself a virgin and brought her along slowly with oral sex and sweetness until, one night, he prostrated her on the wide, comfortable seat of the flyer and tried to put it in her.

That's when they discovered the flaw in Boots' perfect body. The tiny girl had a tiny, uh, thing. Try as he might, Tom could not complete the act of his desire. Try as she might, for liberal portions of oral sex and a hooker of cherry brandy had prepared her, she could not admit him. The evening ended unsatisfactorily with her lying atop Tom, his member between her tightly closed legs. He spewed passion all over her bare fanny.

Naturally, they tried again – and again – and again. They tried for two weeks running and Tom began to get peevish and then, one night when they were both panting with passion, he rammed it to her and it seemed to split her right up the middle and there were copious quantities of blood and unbearable stabs of pain so that she had to fight him off and then she wept all the way home. After that the relationship deteriorated until, finally, she couldn't stand the sight of him because it reminded her of her pain.

Just to prove that she was normal, she seduced a young boy in the neighborhood, a boy whose development was pint-sized, just right for her newly healed tightness. She achieved a weak but satisfactory climax and then she swore off sex entirely until she had access to her first sensualizer in the service.

In the service, the tiny girl with the tiny attributes was discovered to have a massive capacity for holding complicated math in her pretty little head. She was selected to take the exam for entrance to the academy from the ranks, scored high, graduated with the highest marks in math in the history of the establishment and was drafted by computer for service on the exploratory ship *Swinger*. She was, of course, given the opportunity not to follow the computer's choice, but the idea of being a pioneer appealed to her, so she volunteered. Thus she found herself in the company of the staid Captain Asa Smith, the lively, friendly Lt Ellie Martin and she also discovered that two members of the crew were constantly on the make for her.

She was correct with Captain Smith, friendly with Ellie and properly cool to the smooth advances of Lt Knight and the open invitations of Sgt Decker. She felt a little bit sorry for Blackie, knowing as she did that Lt Knight was getting to Lt Martin with regularity, leaving the sergeant only the sensualizer, but she was not about to express her sympathy by letting the brute rip and tear her as Tom had

31

ripped and torn her. Gosh, she'd been weeks healing to the point where she could take a douche without pain.

So, as the big jump approached, as the half-way point neared in their voyage, the situation had established itself. Blackie continued to resent his exclusion from the goodies he was sure the Captain and the Lieutenant enjoyed, John Knight continued to screw Ellie Martin with vigor and regularity. Captain Smith continued to be the strong, silent, faithful type who scorned both sensualizer and the presence of the two nubile girls in his crew, and Boots continued to perform her little acts of masturbatory imagination via the sensualizer.

At J-minus-one, Captain Asa Smith, assembled the crew in control, all at their places. Boots Pastele had been working constantly for twenty-four earthhours, buoyed up by a really jazzy pill administered by the medical officer, to check and recheck through various shipboard computers, the original figures for their jump through space. The drive of the big proton engines had pushed them near the speed of light where strange and wonderful things began to happen. The mass of the *Swinger* was effectively huge, massive to the point of being fantastic. Time did funny things, too. And the frail human body went on and on as if nothing were wrong.

In theory, a space jump was a precise, simple thing. In practice, a million and one things could go wrong. No one actually understood what happened during a space jump, but the results could be determined in advance to a satisfactory degree. In effect, although vastly simplified, to jump in space meant: one, attaining a speed very close to the speed of light; two, hooking on to the gravitational field of a star of known density and whereabouts – in relation to the charted portions of the galaxy; three, using the gravitational field of the star, the pull of the engines and a process known as the Muleholtzen effect to swing out of space and time using the star as an anchor. No one could explain what happened to a ship when it was in a space jump but that didn't matter. Muleholtzen had theorized, back in the old days of space travel, that the ship would eventually be pulled back into space and time by the gravity of the star at a distance roughly equal, but opposed to, the distance from the star at the point of jumping.

The *Swinger* was pointed toward the Orion Arm of the galaxy and was using Alpha Boötes as an anchor and Lt Pastele's painstaking check of the figures showed them to be at the proper point at the proper time. At J-minus-five minutes, the Captain smiled grimly at his crew and began the countdown. John Knight, watching the gauges, which told him his big engines were delivering proper power, stood ready to cut in the Muleholtzen Phaser. Boots minded her computers. The Captain watched his control chronometer. John Knight swallowed nervously. Sometimes ships went into the jump and didn't come out. Ellie Martin, in her medical white one-piece, rode herd on temperature and environment controls and Sergeant Decker stood ready to take over in the event of personnel failure, since a good weapons sergeant knows just about all there is to know about the operation of a ship anyhow.

Asa Smith's voice, calm, commanding, assured, counted, 'Nine-eight-seven-six-five-four-three-two-one – ' and the universe ceased to exist as they swam dizzily in nothingness for what could have been an eternity or a split second while automatic relays timed the firing of the great engines and the duration of the devastating power of the Muleholtzen Phaser and then they were in strange skies with familiar star patterns missing. Into the spiral arm of Orion, stars massive thick around them, so unlike the relatively unpopulated backwoods of the galaxy wherein existed their sun.

33

'My Gawd,' said Blackie Decker.

'You put it very well,' said Captain Asa Smith.

They lived because Earth telescopes and computers and man's brain had devised an avenue for them through the cluttered areas beyond Alpha Boötes. Traveling at a speed only slightly under the speed of light, the ship sped through crowded star fields toward a particular segment of the spiral arm, decelerating now, a process which would require the same amount of time as acceleration, except that strange things had happened to time during the jump so that it was now six months and two and a half weeks ago. By earthtime, the *Swinger* came out of the jump at the exact moment it blasted off from earthstation. Shipboard time, however, continued, so that to the crew, the journey which consumed a year earthtime, assuming that their return would be as uneventful as the outward trip, would be, aboard ship, two long years. One year out, one year back, shiptime.

The jump over, the ship decelerating normally, John Knight breathed a sigh, made necessary adjustments to the engines, the ship having turned during the jump, and felt the negligible thrust of the deceleration against the well-regulated shipboard gravity.

Captain Smith served champagne. He made a small speech designed to bolster the morale of the crew to face the boring six months of deceleration. He served one glass of champagne to each and then went to his quarters to record the successful jump in his log and to write a letter to his wife, who at that very moment was enjoying the carnal thrusts of a Space Marine from Port-au-Prince.

'I got a couple of bottles of this bubbly saved up from my rations,' Sergeant Decker told Lt Pastele. 'I sure would like to share it with someone friendly,' *and soft and willing*, he added under his breath.

'I'm sorry, Sergeant,' Boots said. 'It's been a long haul. I think I'd better rest.'

'You got any of your booze ration left?' John Knight asked Ellie, standing on the other side of the control room, keeping a wary eye on that bastard, Sgt Decker, who, although Knight couldn't hear him, was obviously trying to step across the barriers of rank and put the make on Lt Pastele.

'You gotta be kidding,' Ellie said. 'What do you think that was you were drinking the other night? That was my ration for last week and *this* week.'

'Oh, well,' John said. 'We'll have to console ourselves with liquor for the soul.'

'Hoo boy,' she said grinning. 'You go jump on the sensualizer. I'm wrung out. That was my first jump.'

'Nothing to it,' Knight said, hiding his shaking hands behind him, glancing at Sgt Decker, the bastard, who had finally quit bothering Lt Pastele.

'You say,' Ellie told him. 'But that doesn't stop my butterflies from flying around in my gut. Me for bed.'

'My idea exactly,' John said, smiling seductively.

'Alone. Just me. Without company. Dig?'

'You're a hard-hearted woman, Ellie Martin.' He was, however, a tiny bit relieved. He knew Lt Pastele had been given a jazzum pill to keep her alert and aware during the critical pre-jump period. Jazzum pills always made him sexy. He wondered if they had the same effect on the blonde lieutenant. He proceeded to inquire, indirectly. He walked up behind Lt Pastele, who was now alone with him in the control room, both Sgt Decker and Lt Martin having taken their leave. He put his hand gently on her bare elbow and she jumped as if she had been shocked.

'Sorry,' she said, 'guess I'm still keyed up.'

'Jazzum does take a while to wear off,' he said. 'I have just the remedy for it, however. Lt Knight's massage

35

service, guaranteed to relax the tightest muscles and countereffect the stimulation of jazzum pills until the subject is sleeping like a babe.'

'Thanks, Lieutenant, but I think I'll go to my quarters and ask Ellie for a counterstimulant.'

'You're missing out on something which I'm told is very grand,' John said, disappointed.

'A rain check, Lieutenant,' Boots said, very formal, as she left Knight alone in the control room.

'Hey,' John yelled after her, 'who's supposed to be on watch? It's not my trick.'

'It's mine,' Boots called after her, 'but I've been up for twenty-four hours. Captain said to draft someone to fill in. You're it, Lieutenant.'

Christ, he thought, sitting down. Ellie bugged out. Boots uncooperative as usual. And now stuck with the duty when it wasn't his trick. Hell, going down to the R & R beat pulling someone else's duty.

5

Jacuandapentathelemethorilide, popularly known as jazzum, was a drug developed in the Muleholtzen labs back on Earth. It extended the lasting qualities of the human body almost indefinitely without serious harm. It was also the most effective aphrodisiac in existence. It was extremely popular among the flyer set, who believed in burning candles at both ends and in the middle, and it was used in industry and service with the tacit approval of those in authority, although nowhere in regulations could one find a mention of the drug. Its use was accepted because it allowed frail human bodies to extend themselves far beyond normal endurance in the performance of vital tasks. The stage of the technology had long since passed human ability to keep up with machines and jazzum was considered, by most military commanders, to be a vital part of his logistics in any complicated mission. The sexually stimulating portions of the effects of the drug were regrettable. Back at the Muleholtzen labs, that vast complex of scientific factories which had grown from the genius of one now-dead old man, thousands of scientists worked almost constantly to weed out the aphrodisiac effects and leave only the ability-extending properties of the drug. One young technician in Detroit made a jazzum derivative which kept only the aphrodisiac effect and it was so powerful that he, after testing a minute quantity of the drug, lost himself in the most expensive whorehouse in Chicago's Loop and stayed there for six days, setting a record of performance which left hardened pros gasping. But no one, to the date, had been able to make jazzum with just the desirable – from the command viewpoint – effects.

The only thing which allowed jazzum to be used on vital missions was the fact that the sexy properties of the drug were, somehow, completely ineffective in situations of stress. Thus, when Lt Pastele was concerned about the calculations prior to the jump, there was no hint of sexuality in her. However, once the tension of the situation was past, good old jazzum went its licentious way and, by the time Boots made her way to her quarters she had a champion case of hot pants.

The room shared by the two female officers was, by necessity, small. It contained a desk and chair and the two automated bunks. Over the desk was a microfilm viewer flanked by two shelves of filmed books. In the walls were lockers containing the few personal effects allowed, spare uniforms and emergency breathing equipment. The bath was a tiny cubicle lined with a soft, yielding plastic. There was room between the two bunks for walk space and not much more. However, the small room had its luxuries. Music was available from the ship's master musicvault either on a room-wide basis or individually through earphones. The entire ceiling could be turned into a viewscreen on which could be played the top productions of Earth film companies. The bunks, themselves, were automated marvels of engineering which could be restful beds or energetic exercisers.

The room, like the entire ship, was a technological marvel. It was instrumented to warn of any change in environment. So closely was it controlled that a change of three degrees in body temperature would register on instruments, thus warning the ship's doctor, Ellie Martin, that a crew member had a fever. And, in addition to all of the other instrumentation which was a part of the crew's quarters, there was, high up, a little square viewscreen which was almost always dead, for it was the central scan system of the ship, wired directly into command and available only to the officer in charge. During emergencies, the command post could scan every inch of the ship. There were infrequent tests of the system, routine tests which were presaged by the words, 'This is the Captain. In ten minutes, at XXXX hours, there will be a routine test of the shipscan system.' At the appointed time, all hands having been warned so that they would not be surprised, a warning buzzer would sound and the little screen, although there would be no visible change, would come to life. The buzzer would sound at regular intervals during the screen's operation; for privacy, in an overcrowded world, had become man's most precious possession and not even the service dared to or cared to intrude into the privacy of individuals. Every ship in the space fleet had shipscan. Not once in the history of the system had shipscan been used improperly. Although every man aboard a ship lived with shipscan daily, hourly, no man ever gave it a thought because everyone knew that they were allowed complete privacy in their own quarters. They also knew that shipscan was equipped with a double-fail-safe guard which prevented anyone, even the commanding officer, from spying on any portion of the ship without first giving and continuing to give warning via the buzzer. No one had ever tried to circumvent the fail-safe system of shipscan, or at least, no one had ever been successful.

Not until Blackie Decker, pissed-off because all that good nookie was being kept in officer country, began to tinker with the mechanisms on the pretext of checking the armament wares of the *Swinger*. He came upon his idea by accident, while doing some legitimate preventive maintenance. He found the fail-safe box for the shipscan system and thought nothing of it until later. When the possibilities occurred to him, he shrugged them off. Hell, no one could subvert the fail-safe system. That, however, roused his pride. He was a techman. Techmen put the damned fail-safe system together, so a good techman could take it apart.

And if he could take it apart, he could bypass the buzzer system and, maybe, wire the whole rig into his personal viewscreen in his quarters and – but what the hell, what good would that do? He'd be able to watch the Captain take a piss and watch the broads undress, but watching a naked broad on a viewscreen was not exactly an experience in days when the human body was a common, ordinary, arty but plentiful sight everywhere. They started with topless bathing suits back in the twentieth century and had worked up to permissive nude bathing by the year two-thousand. Most broads still wore something on public beach, simply because of practical things. Like the first ape that put a fig leaf over his privates to keep the mosquitoes from chewing his balls, the modern world stuck to clothing because sand in a naked twat makes like a cement mixer. Then, too, there was something about the womanly nude, which was made more mysterious, more appealing, by the addition of a wisp of cloth here and there, so some broads bathed in the nude and attracted less attention than those who bathed in artfully contrived bikinis.

But it wasn't the mere thought of seeing the two females nude which caused Blackie to start tinkering with the shipscan. He had a damned good idea that John Knight was throwing it to one or both of the broads and he didn't like being left out. He went back to the fail-safe box out of bitterness, with a half-formed plan to get that bastard Knight and, maybe, to get, in a different and more interesting way, one or both of the female officers. He found that techmen had, indeed, installed the fail-safe and that it was vastly overrated. The reason no one had ever subverted the system before – if, indeed, no one ever had – was because no qualified techman ever really wanted to.

It took a while, for he had to work carefully for fear of discovery. He didn't know the penalties for intrusion into personal privacy, but he figured that they would at least match those of forcible rape, which had been increased, in the past decade, from six months to a year in a World Psychhospital. He didn't like the idea of spending time at all in a psychward, with nuts probing around in his brain and changing things. He sort of liked himself the way he was. But he felt very put-upon. That bastard, Knight, was getting his every day and just because they were officers didn't mean that they had to exclude Blackie Decker from their fun and games.

It happened that Blackie completed his wire-in to his viewscreen the day before the big jump. He wasn't interested in spying on J-day, because the big J made all things else unimportant, but after the jump he had time on his hands. He went to his room to relax a bit from the tension and thought about his new playtoy. All he had to do was throw a switch and then select any portion of the ship he wanted to see. He fell down onto his bunk, adjusted the controls, flipped the switch which put the shipscan on his screen – a large screen covering the entire ceiling of the two man quarters which he occupied alone, as the only enlisted man aboard. Lt Ellie Martin, in her white uniform, was sitting in her adjusted bunk. Blackie turned on the shipscan just in time to see Boots Pastele come in the door. For a long time nothing much happened. Then it was the damndest thing Blackie had ever seen.

'Gawd,' Boots said, 'I'm glad that's over.' She drew the back of her hand across her forehead wearily and brought it away moist. She knew that, in the absolutely perfect temperature of the ship, her perspiration was strictly of the nervous variety.

'You were tremendous, Boots,' Ellie said in sincere admiration. 'I don't think anyone in the service could have done a better job.'

'I'm just glad we have a few months before I have to do it again,' Boots said, flopping down onto her bunk only to sit up quickly. She felt mentally tired, but her body was keyed up to a point of excitement which startled her. 'Doc, I think you'd better give me something.'

Ellie laughed. 'Getting to you now, huh?' She waved a hand toward the bath. 'I have it ready. The pink pill, then the blue one. Glass of water.' She was still smiling as the blonde moved hurriedly into the bath.

Boots came out, wiping her mouth. There was the most tremendous urge in her. It was a bigger urge than she'd ever felt with Tom. It was bigger, even, than the urge she'd felt when she seduced the neighborhood boy. She paced restlessly up and down the narrow space between the bunks. Ellie watched with some amusement. 'First trip on jazzum?'

'Gawd, yes,' Boots said. 'How long does it take for the counterstimulant to take effect?'

'Good ole jazzum,' Ellie said. 'You have about an hour, at least, before you'll begin to settle down. Maybe more. Sometimes the first time takes longer.'

'Oh, Gawd,' Boots said, giggling suddenly, because she felt the points of her nipples rubbing against the smooth material of her uniform and it was decidedly erotic.

'I'd advise a trip to R & R,' Ellie said. 'Spend the hour in pleasant mental debauchery.'

Boots considered it. It gave her a swift shot of passion to think of the sensualizer, to think of the things she could imagine for herself under the electronic hood. Then she frowned. What the hell was wrong? Something. Something in her was telling her that the sensualizer was artificial and what she needed was the real thing. She was shocked into motionless wonder. She sat down, adjusted the bunk to support her knees.

'No sensualizer, huh?' Ellie asked.

'I dunno,' Boots said. 'Gosh, I feel so funny.'

'Yeah, I know. Ole jazzum make it glow, baby. Makes the sensualizer seem like pretty tame stuff, huh?' Boots looked at her quickly. It was sometimes uncomfortable living in close quarters with a psych doctor. She didn't like another person knowing as much of her as she knew, herself. 'Well, honey, there's always old mother nature's remedy.'

Boots felt herself blush. She knew that Ellie meant screwing with a real man and she knew, also, that the statement was as close as Ellie had come to admitting what Boots suspected, that she was having an affair with John Knight. The blush faded quickly, however, to be replaced with a strong urge to seek out Knight, throw him onto the ground and rape him. Among the things which kept her from doing it was the very real fear of the pain she would have because of her smallness. She sighed, tossed, turned onto her stomach with her face to the wall.

'You gonna lay there and suffer?' Ellie asked. When she got no answer, she rose and sat on the edge of Boots' bed.

'Look, I know how you feel. I been there myself. Why don't you do as I say, take a ride on the sensualizer?'

'Oh, shit,' Boots said.

'OK, suit yourself.' She started to leave, then her fondness for the girl asserted itself. Then, too, she was a doctor and one of her charges was in distress. 'Here,' she said, putting her hands on Boots' neck and rubbing, 'this will help a little.'

'You don't have to,' Boots said, weakly. Strong soft hands kneaded the taut muscles along her neck. She felt like purring with the goodness of it.

'All for the good of the service,' Ellie said, extending her massage down Boots' back, working on knotted muscles with the knowledge of one who knew the human body from the inside out. 'Feel good?'

'Ummmm,' Boots said.

'But it won't put out the fire.' She worked. She could feel Boots relaxing slightly. She thought about the girl with a professional interest. There was no great cause for concern, but Boots' refusal to avail herself of the release offered by the sensualizer was unusual. Most people, coming off jazzum, rushed to the nearest bed or the nearest R & R room.

It was Ellie's job, as medofficer of the *Swinger*, to spot abnormalities in her charges and remedy them. 'Hey, kid,' she said, 'how do you feel?'

'OK.'

'Hot pants?'

'Ummmmm.'

'Don't be ashamed of it. It's normal. But I gotta say some things.'

Boots heard the slight change in Ellie's tone, the alternation of her voice which indicated that Ellie was serious. 'What have you got against R & R?'

'Nothing,' Boots said, 'nothing at all. I use it once a week, as in the regulations.'

'Kid, it's not too cool to try to come off jazzum cold turkey.'

'Oh,' Boots said. 'So that's it.' She turned, pulling out from under Ellie's hands. 'You're making an official inquiry?'

'An off the record official inquiry. Let's keep it informal. Just between us girls, you know. You got a hangup?'

44

'You have my records,' Boots said, somewhat indignantly.

'Sure, sure. Normal. Normal sexual tendencies. Presumed sexual experience slight, etc.' She pushed Boots back down, rolled her over, and began the massage again. 'But you're steaming. You're a human being and jazzum affects all human beings. Yet you won't go to the sensualizer. Why?'

She knew she had to answer. Ellie was the medofficer. 'Well, it's, I don't know, it seems so – so – '

'Artificial? So masturbatory?'

'Well, yes.'

'How much experience have you had, Boots?'

'Do I have to answer?'

'No, but I'd like for you to. I'm responsible for you, both your physical and mental health. I'd hate like hell for you to get hung up on sex or something and blow the big jump on the way home.'

'Don't worry. I'll be all right.'

'Look, Boots. I'm the medofficer and I'm your friend. And I have a vested interest in your peace of mind. Now let's talk about sex and why you're so hung up you won't take the release offered by the sensualizer.'

Boots sighed. 'Is that an order, doctor?' At least it was taking her mind off the increasingly urgent need of her loins.

'An order,' Ellie said.

'OK. I have a shameful past. I slept with two men – uh – boys.'

'Well, what were they? Men or boys?'

'A bit of both,' Boots said. 'One was quite young and the other was older.'

'Was it satisfactory?'

'Well, yes and no,' Boots said, feeling the soothing hands still kneading her tense muscles. 'All right, hell, I

45

guess I do have a bit of a hangup.' She took a deep breath. After all, Ellie was a qualified doctor, trained in both physical and psych medicine. It was about time she told someone. So she did. In his quarters, just forward of the engine room, Sgt Blackie Decker listened with sudden interest and chuckled. Christ, he thought, if that was her only problem, he would fix that real quick. All that chick needed was a good reaming out and then funsville. In the officers' quarters, female division, Ellie listened with interest and patience.

'That is not the insurmountable problem you think it is,' Ellie told her. 'Let me take a look.'

'Now?' Boots asked.

'Why not?' She zipped Boots' one-piece and bared a set of nice, rounded breasts. It was unfashionable to wear a bra and Boots was no exception to the rule. Modern day thinking was that artificial support of the breasts caused a permanent relaxation of the muscles. In the past, women were so eager to close off their breasts that they started their little girls in training bras even before there was anything to train. Modern mothers didn't put bras on kids, let the breasts grow naturally, let the firm, natural muscle tone develop and hold the breasts in natural attitudes.

Boots wore government issue panties, sturdy, practical things, white and neat. 'Off with them,' Ellie told her, very businesslike. She came off with her panties and lay on the bunk, legs open, for the very informal examination. Ellie put her hands down between a set of very nice thighs, pale white, looking natural and never sunburned, and her fingers probed, caught little petals of flesh, parted them, exposed the white, iris-like opening. 'Humm.'

An unsuspected sensuality was present. Boots felt like yelling, her need was so great. The touch of the doctor's

46

fingers was a tickling itch which made her want to climb the walls.

In his quarters, Blackie, via the shipscan, had a good tri-vee view of the tiniest twat he'd ever seen.

'You do have problems,' Ellie said, her fingers probing, pushing one deeply into the iris-flower opening and testing. Boots flinched, but it was not painful, just maddeningly stimulating. 'Have to do something about this, unless you want to spend the rest of your life socializing with midgets.'

'I don't know about doing something about it,' Boots said, 'but if you don't stop *that*, something very immediate might happen.'

Ellie giggled. 'That bad?' Just to tease her friend, she pressed her palm, hard, down on a swollen little jewel of sensation. Without conscious movement, Boots' loins rose to meet the caress. Then, realizing what she'd done, she pulled back. 'You are in a bad way,' Ellie said.

At first it was like a game to Ellie. It was funny, in a dear sort of way. She knew how Boots felt, having been keyed up by jazzum in the past. She knew that there was only one cure for the jazzum itch and that was orgasm, maybe several of them. In a teasing sort of way, she toyed with a bit of erectile tissue which was gorged with blood and studded with nerve ends.

'Hey,' Boots said, pushing at the hand, trying to sit up. But she was in the full grip of passion, drug stimulated and heightened. When Ellie playfully pushed her back, her hand between Boots' breasts, Boots lay back feebly.

'I could do it for you,' Ellie said, still feeling teasy and playful. She rubbed.

The sound which Boots made was eerie in its intensity. The violent, bucking, thrusting movement of her loins was sex and pure sex and the strength of it made Ellie tingle a bit, as if some of the passion in Boots' body were

47

bleeding out into her own. She rubbed with her hand, smooth thighs came together to clasp her arm in a strong vice and the lithe, smooth body under her eyes heaved up once, twice, again and again and then she knew with certainty, with her own pulse pounding in sympathy, that Boots was being climaxed, was peaking with grunts and moans of pleasure.

'Again,' Boots moaned, the first peak being only an appetizer in her state of arousal. 'Oh, God, Ellie, again!'

Ellie licked full lips musingly, seeking the upthrust loins, the exposed, tiny womanspot, the lovehair and the long, silken thighs and she was knowledgeable enough to know that her feelings, then, were not abnormal. Normal women can be interested in the bodies of other women under certain circumstances. Homosexuality, as a sickness, had been long since conquered. That it still existed, among certain libertine types, testified only to the fact that the world was permissive of personal pleasures and that the human body, especially the body of a beautiful woman, was an art object.

'Please, Ellie,' the blonde begged, beside herself, 'please.'

'All right,' Ellie said, nodding, 'but it's going to cost you.

'Oh, anything! Please!'

'I mean, I'm not a block of ice,' Ellie said. 'It's gotta go both ways, hear?'

'Yes,' Boots whispered, eyes wide as Ellie zipped her uniform and came out of it, blue panties following soon. 'What do you want me to do?'

'Just what comes naturally, lover,' Ellie said, leaning to place her elongated, full breasts atop Boots' rounded, smaller ones. 'Just what comes naturally.'

What came completely naturally was a full-mouthed kiss with swapping tongues and with Ellie, thunder coming from deep inside, licking the small, pretty mouth of the blonde with a hunger which added to the fire in Boots' blood. What came natural was a mutual seeking out of breasts with shaking hands, shared emotions and shared pleasure as feminine fingers fondled feminine nipples knowingly and lips were wet and hungry. First it was Ellie, bending, her rump pointed out in the room, making for a spectacular view on the shipscan for Sgt Blackie Decker, who was now possessed of a massive erection.

It was the damndest thing he'd ever seen. He'd heard of it and in some places they still ran shows with two girls, but he'd never fancied it. He'd never wasted a credit buying sex, since there was plenty of it running around for free, much less wasting money on sex shows. But here he was watching avidly as Lt Martin made passionate love to Lt Pastele.

Ellie found the feel of a nipple in her mouth to be erotic as all hell. She promptly placed her breast – her left breast was more sensitive – into the little mouth of Boots Pastele and moaned with pleasure when little white teeth nibbled lovingly at the small, protruding member.

Meanwhile, body to body, Boots was heaving, mound to mound, reaching, reaching until, with a sound, half cry and half laugh, she reached her second peak.

'I should have popped a jazzum myself,' Ellie said, envying the ability of the girl to come back so quickly, not even slowed by the climax. She felt that it was time to do *something*. She knew the woman-woman bit, but it was new to her. It was pleasant and sort of exciting to hold Boots in her arms, but she needed something else.

'OK, kid,' Ellie said.

'Ummmmmmk,' Boots moaned, heaving under her again.

49

'This is fine,' Ellie said, 'but it doesn't cut the mustard. Let's do the whole bit?'

'Hummm?' Boots moaned.

'I mean the whole bit,' she said, putting her hand between them, finding the wet-hot little area. 'Like kiss-kiss-kiss.'

'There?' Boots croaked.

'Where else honey?' She shifted on the bed. 'You first, doll. It's my turn.'

'Oh, I can't!'

'I'll slug you. You got me churned up good, doll. I ain't about to take it to the sensualizer.'

'Oh, I can't,' Boots repeated.

'Goddamned right you can. Look, I'll do it first. Then you.' Suiting action to words, she flung herself down, pushed her face into Boots' lap, found sweet, hot thighs against her cheeks and felt the little body rise to meet her. It wasn't bad. She extended a tongue tentatively and tasted the smoothness and Boots jerked with bliss and pressed it hot and wet against her mouth and then she gave it to her, tongue moving like fire while Boots peaked immediately, screaming delight.

'All right, damnit,' Ellie said. She positioned herself, sat on Boots' face and felt it. 'Like I did,' she whispered, and the tongue came out.

Boots, still flying on jazzum, worked with a will, quickly bringing Ellie to the heights. Boots received still another thrill when, with a muffled sound of lust, Ellie twisted, fell, worked into the mutual position and began trading sensations until, with a universe ending bang, Ellie came and Boots hit the top for still another time and they both fell onto their sides, exhausted.

It was the damndest thing Blackie had ever seen. He was so hot he felt like playing with it like a kid. He wished feverishly to be in officer's country so he could solve all their problems by reaming out that little one and giving Ellie all she could take, too.

'Oh, Ellie,' Boots said, weakly, tiredly, 'are we so terrible?'

'Only if you think we are,' Ellie said. 'We're free, adult and responsible. That's not my kick, ordinarily, but I'll have to admit that you had me going there. You'd better watch out or I'll be feeding you jazzum all the time.'

Boots giggled. 'I don't think I could stand it. I'm *killed*.'

''Bout time. I thought you were going to go on into a permanent orgasm.'

'Wouldn't that be lovely?' Boots asked. 'I guess I am terrible.'

'Then I'll have to put you through a complete psych treatment. I mean it about the hangups. I got a stake in you getting us back home through that last, homeward jump. Look, it's no more than sex between man and woman. I'm not going to go through life lusting for you and I don't think you will lust for me, not after we fix you up.'

'Fix me up?' Boots asked sleepily, the counterstimulant beginning to work at last.

'Little minor surgery, Boots. Fix it so the next time you're with a man you'll find out what it really is about.'

'Oh, I don't think so. Not while we're on a trip.'

'When could you think of a better time? Look, it'll take all of twenty minutes. I got the equipment and the knowledge. A little snip with the knife and, whamo, you're a full-fledged woman. Two weeks to heal and you're ready for anything.'

'Like Lt Knight?' Boots asked, unable to contain her curiosity any longer.

'What are you, some kind of spy fink?'

'Well, I – '

'OK, I confess. Look, it's not all that bad. It's against

51

regulations, but people have been breaking regulations since the first Army was organized. You might follow my example. Knight is a good one. Knows his stuff and no emotional involvements expected. You might give it a whirl yourself after I fix you up a bit. Do you good.'

In his quarters, Sgt Decker cursed in a low voice. That bastard wasn't going to get that sweet little twat. If anyone got it it would be Blackie Decker. He hoped that the doctor woman wouldn't make it *too* big. He liked 'em tight.

Boots chuckled sleepily. 'I wonder what our Captain would say if he knew his medofficer was advising his navigation officer to go to bed with a man.'

'I'd hate to hear it,' Ellie said. She went into the bath and when she came out Boots was sleeping, legs akimbo, womanhood gleaming with moisture and signs of passionate use.

6

Lt Pastele's minor surgery went off without a hitch. Actually, Lt Martin, medofficer, could have performed the operation with a lazerblade, but Lt Martin, psychdoctor, realized the psychological importance of the patient's decision and gave the minor venture into corrective surgery all the trappings of a far more important operation. It was three earthweeks after the big jump.

During the three week period, Lt Pastele was withdrawn, quieter than usual. Ellie did some probing to see if the rather erotic method she'd used to release Boots from the sexual tensions of the jazzum pill had left Boots suffering from guilt. She got just enough information to know without a doubt that it wasn't the interlude into the ancient rites of Lesbos which had Boots shook. She discovered that Boots, the small girl with the small vaginal opening, was concerned about the operation, which Ellie had scheduled, using her authority as medofficer to leave Boots no choice.

Ellie went into the film room, taking a tiny capsule which contained all that the service had ever been able to find out about Boots Pastele and discovered the background of neoreligion.

'Shucks,' Ellie said, going no deeper into the small girl's background. She immediately changed her argument, telling Boots that the operation would be necessary, anyhow, at some later date when Boots met Mr Right and decided to take a leave of absence from the service to enjoy the permitted two years of marriage and child birthing. As a Space Force officer, Boots would be allowed to produce replacements for herself and her husband, one boy and one girl, carefully programmed gene-wise to combine the very best of both parents.

This was the button. She had merely pushed the wrong one when she'd advised Boots to get laid, presumably by the virile Lt Knight. By playing on the marriage thing she changed Boots's subconscious thinking about the operation entirely. Boots had been looking on the operation as a permissive thing, an evil thing which would open the way to complete debauchery. Now, however, she began to think of the operation as a necessity, something which had to be done sooner or later in order for her to be able, at some later date, to fulfill her function as a woman.

So Ellie, knowing that the human mind is a strange and wonderful thing, went about preparations as if she were performing a holy office. She had Boots dress in a short, white overthing which came to her navel. That left a lot of Boots revealed. Ellie stationed her on an examination table, her heels in the stirrups, legs wide apart and vaginal area exposed. Boots was a bit nervous. When Ellie came at her with a spray can of sanitary depilatory she tried to pull her knees together and found that it was impossible. She was spread so wide she felt that a small groundcar could have been driven between her legs.

'Is that really necessary?' Boots asked, as the spray hit her pubic mound, cool, bracing.

'Not really,' Ellie said. 'Just a precaution.' The spray was already working, dissolving the ash-blonde hairs into a sudsy mass which could be wiped off.

'Well, if it isn't really necessary,' Boots said.

'Too late, baby,' Ellie told her. 'You're bald as a glans penis.'

'Boy,' Boots giggled, 'now I know how your mind works.'

'Actually, you're not bad bald,' Ellie said, finishing

54

wiping away the sudsy depilatory mess and cleaning the area with a mild solution of quanticillion fluid. She splashed the clear, pleasant-smelling liquid down over the plump *labia*, then spread them with her fingers. She worked without gloves, for the quanticillion's fantastic germ-killing power did away with the necessity of her scrubbing up and using rubber gloves. The little flower of whitish tissue inside the *introitus* pulsed reflexively as she splashed quanticillion on it, into it. She quickly spewed plenty of quanticillion into the vaginal passage with a spray container.

'Baby,' she said, smiling, 'you've been skipping the sensualizer sessions.'

'Oh, no,' Boots said guiltily.

'Then why are you responding to my very scientific twiddling of your twat?'

'Oh, Ellie,' Boots said.

'But you are. Your Bartholin glands are functioning.'

'What?' Boots asked, nervously.

'You're creaming your jeans,' Ellie said. 'Making lubrication. Like as if you were going to get laid or something.'

'Well,' Boots said.

'Well, you're not getting laid,' Ellie laughed. 'You're going to be laid open a tiny bit, but that's all.'

In his quarters, where he'd been spending more and more time lately, Blackie Decker told himself that the medical lieutenant was both right and wrong. Maybe Boots wasn't going to get laid right that minute, but as soon as she was layable after the operation, Blackie was going to have her or know the reason why. He was stretched out on his bunk, looking up into the large screen of the shipscan system, a system he'd subverted against all regulations and all standards of decent behaviour. In the weeks since he'd accidentally tuned in to see the two female officers servicing each other in their quarters, he'd watched eagerly for a repeat of the scene but, to his disappointment, had seen nothing out of the ordinary. Oh, three or four times he'd tuned in on Knight and Martin screwing like minks, but watching that bastard, Knight, throw it to Martin wasn't his bag. He just got mad to see all that freckled woman being punched by that old, grey-headed sonofabitch. At first he tried to imagine himself servicing Ellie instead of Knight, but that made him mad, too. He would watch them shuck out of their pants and go at it, Ellie's thin waist encircled by Knight's arms, her small ass humping under Knight's thrusts and it would make him steam with anger. Knight was a sonofabitch and Ellie was a bitch for letting that sonofabitch screw her and then turning up her nose at the lowly sergeant. Sometimes Blackie felt like grabbing the bitch in the hall or somewhere and throwing it to her. He seriously considered blackmail. He could go up to her and say, 'Look, sweetie, I got the word. You and that bastard, Knight, are making it like rabbits all over the ship, in the medroom, in the engine room, in Knight's quarters. Now you put out a little for old Blackie or we'll see what the Captain has to say about this.'

But Blackie had never been forced to buy his sex and blackmail was just a form of buying. So he watched Knight and Martin screw with all the decorations – like Ellie taking that bastard's dick into her smiling mouth and like that. He watched and he steamed and he made a firm resolution that the other one was his. That bastard, Knight, could have the prick-sucking Ellie. He'd take that little blonde one with the little twat.

Which was about to be made not so little under his very eyes. Well, not exactly under his very eyes, but at least under the eye of the shipscan system, which had become Blackie's eye.

'I'm sorry,' Boots said. 'I don't mean to react. It's just that when you – '

'When I rub your clit?' Ellie said, smiling and suiting actions to words.

'Stop it,' Boots said, wiggling in the examination saddle.

'In a way,' Ellie mused, still playing idly with the now-distended twit of clit above Boots' slash, 'it's a damned shame. It is by far the nicest little pussy I've seen.'

'Yeah, yeah,' Blackie Decker said, down in his quarters, zipping open his one-piece and grabbing his massive erection in both hands like a baseball bat. A full inch stuck over the top, and he was a man with big hands.

'You're teasing me,' Boots said. 'I'm all right. You don't have to use a bedside manner on me. I'm fine.'

'But hardly functional for the purpose for which it was intended,' Ellie said, still fingering the fine little ball of nerves while Boots bit her lip to keep from flinging her bottom up to press into the caress. 'So, my love, we'd best be on with it.' So saying, she reached for a spray can of local anesthetic.

'You're not going to do it while I'm awake?' Boots asked, panic in her voice.

'Aw, honey, you won't feel a thing. You'll be so dead down here that the sexiest man on earth couldn't make you feel a thing.'

'But I'm a notorious coward, Ellie,' Boots said. 'I think I'd rather have a general.'

Ellie considered it. 'Well,' she said, 'I'll compromise for hypnosis.'

'I – I guess that would be all right.'

'Then go to sleep,' Ellie said, making mysterious signs with her fingers in front of Boots' face, lowering her voice to seductive depths. 'Sleep, little bird, and feel no pain.' Boots let her eyes close. Smilingly, Ellie pinched one of

57

the white thighs on the inside and there was no response. She hummed busily as she prepared a lazerblade, grateful, at least, that she was not going to have to use a bloody knife after all. 'Sleep little bird,' she hummed, setting up the lazer machine between Boots' outflung legs. Because the operation was of so much psychic importance to the patient, she'd been prepared to go the entire route, make a neat incision, show the patient some bloody rags, etc. Now she could do it neatly and quickly and bloodlessly with the beam and it would be finished. She checked the depth penetration setting, focused the beam, sighted along the barrel of the machine to the spot of impact – the white iris of the opening. 'My God,' she said.

She looked at the exposed, bald pelvis, the soft, ruby tinted labia, the little, tiny, small, wee opening and she remembered the dear taste of the girl under her mouth. Well, soon it would belong to mankind, not just to a sympathetic psychdoctor. She truly regretted the loss.

But it was not a total loss, not yet! She shoved the lazer out of the way hurriedly, cranked the table until the exposed, opened slit was even with her smiling mouth, leaned forward and kissed it tenderly. Then, tongue working rapidly, she snaked her hand inside her one-piece, down into her bikini blue panties and fingered herself, feeling the beginning flow of glandular activity as she kissed and rubbed and worked herself into a quite glorious climax before she stood back, smiling and pant-ing, to look at the now-used opening which had felt her tongue.

In his quarters, Blackie Decker looked at the opening also and spouted the first totally manual spout he'd spouted since he found out what girls were for.

In the medroom, the medofficer, panties wet with passion juice, resterilized the patient and exposed a bit of tender flesh to a lazerblade for a fraction of a second and Boots Pastele no longer had problems.

But it was still small. Blackie could look at it and see that it was still small. He would have killed that medbitch if she'd made it too large.

'Wake up, Boots,' Ellie said, snapping her fingers.

Boots sat up, pulling her heels out of the stirrups. 'I dreamed I was getting a climax,' she whispered, looking around with a dazed expression.

'Well,' Ellie said, her eyes sparkling mischievously, 'hypnosis is a funny thing.'

'Is it all over?'

'All done. Simple, really. You'll have a bit of soreness for a few days, but in a couple of weeks you'll be ready for anything.'

'Well,' Boots said, visions of sheer lust leaping into her head, visions involving the handsome Lt Knight.

And in his quarters, Blackie Decker also had his visions. And he made a mark on his calendar. Two weeks to F-Day. He counted the day of the operation as the first day.

7

Far, far behind them, and getting further away each second, Alpha Boötes twinkled, a small star lost in the glory of the crowded Orion Arm, which surrounded them. John Knight's huge engines roared and throbbed, never still, never silent, fighting the frightful inertia of their speed, slowing the ship gradually as the big star fields fought against the steering engines, tugging this way and that. It was touchy. Navigation inside the field of a spiral arm was a complication which needed centuries of computer research compacted into the shipboard brains. Lt Boots Pastele, near-genius, used every minute of her watch time, and not a little of what was supposed to be her own time, checking one computer against the other, checking, rechecking, making up for her inexperience in actual field conditions with diligent effort.

Ahead of them, detected by ultra-sensitive instruments back on Earth, confirmed by field probes run by ships nearer the Orion Arm, was an insignificant little class C star, their destination. They had traveled light years and risked the vast uncertainties of the Muleholtzen jump to reach that small star, because, as the art of space travel progressed from the primitive rockets of the 1960's, as instrumentation improved, as man began to make a search for the source of the flying saucers, in short, began to want to find out if he were alone in the universe, it was discovered that a sun having planets was a rare, rare thing. Old Sol, with its family, was perhaps a oner. Nowhere near, not within fifty light-years, was there another planet system. When it became apparent that planets were, seemingly, confined to our solar system, the art of space travel was almost abandoned. Man walked on the moon and Mars, died in the vapors of Venus and circled the maelstrom of Saturn and there was no place to go. All was hostile and alien and it seemed, until Muleholtzen revolutionized the world and space travel, that man would be a stay-at-home, now and forever.

Then Muleholtzen developed the Phaser. A man named Silas Swamper invented a variation of the radio-telescope which spotted no less than two hundred planet families, not one of which was within hailing distance of the Earth. The urge to find kind, to find other beings living in the vastness of the star fields sent the little exploration ships shooting out. After searching fifty-five planet systems there was a growing feeling of desperation, for the only living thing to be found was a small silicone-life-system bug found on a torrid, airless planet halfway across the galaxy from Earth. However, the riches brought back, in the form of diamonds, which were in short supply on Earth, helped keep the exploration program going. Then, too, there was a growing sentiment among Earth's teeming billions for what a madman called Adolf Hitler had called *lebensraum* – living room, space to live, space to own and space in which to have children. On Earth, having children was not automatic, it was a privilege which was severely controlled by the world government, for if the race had been allowed to breed at the rate which it had reached in the twentieth century, there would not have been room to stand without stepping on someone's foot.

So the little ships flashed outward from old Earth, and the *Swinger*, pegged on Alpha Boötes, shot straight-line perfect down the preplanned alley amid stars toward a class C sun which owned a family of five planets.

As deceleration continued and the minor operation in

a very intimate part of the anatomy of Boots Pastele healed, Sgt Blackie Decker checked off the days on his calendar. Medofficer Ellie Martin watched her friend and noted that the little blonde had made two trips to the sensualizer in one week. Capt. Asa Smith maintained his aloof, proud iron-hard will and wet his sheets with natural wet dreams, dreams which centered around his wife, Elenore, for Capt. Smith was true to his wife even in his dreams. Lt Knight continued to dip his dork in the melting pot of Lt Martin, mainly because Ellie, being a naturally sensuous broad, had come to expect her servicing and demanded it. She didn't yell, 'Screw me, you fink,' but she didn't have to. Any woman who showed passion to John Knight was offering a challenge. The fact that John Knight was bored stiff with Ellie had nothing to do with it. While he lusted for fresh meat, with his eye on the ash-blonde navigation officer, he gritted his even teeth and drove it home to Lt Martin every time she cornered him.

As for Boots, she was having a battle inside herself. The operation, she told herself, was for the future. It had been performed because it was convenient to perform it on a long exploration cruise, there being nothing else to do, so that she could, when she met the right man, take her turn at holding the population of the race at status quo by producing two scientifically perfect offspring. It was not, as her body insisted, performed so that she could rape Lt Knight.

Yet, her body talked to her. She would find herself dripping for it while on watch; she'd feel a suspicious dampness in her sensible service panties and realize that she'd been daydreaming about some faceless man. This sudden onset of lust scared her and drove her to the sensualizer. Lt Martin saw her go twice in one week. Actually, she had made three more visits to the R & R room of which Lt Martin was ignorant. Each time she hooked in, brought out a faceless man, and screwed him blue in the faceless face with multiple orgasms. And each time she came closer and closer to having John Knight take the place of the faceless lover and each time, in her mind-created debauchery, she let the organ of the male lover grow a bit until she was taking, in her sensualized frenzy, a tool which would once have split her wide open, would have been more painful and shameful than the oversized cookie of Tom, her first love, the boy she had given herself to so eagerly only to be hurt frightfully.

Blackie kept track of Boots by shipscan and he knew how often she'd been to the sensualizer. He was toying with a plan to hook his room circuits into the sensualizer system for the purpose of sharing Boots Pastele's sexual dreams, but he decided it was too risky. He didn't want to go screwing around with a circuitry which was concerned intimately with a human's brain, for the sensualizer worked in strange and mysterious ways. Then, too, he had only four days to wait until the blonde lieutenant's snatch was healed. He didn't have any solidly formed plans, but he was going to have her even if he had to reach out into the corridor and drag her into his room and rape hell out of her.

At F-day minus three, three days before the day marked on Blackie's calendar, medofficer Ellie Martin spoke to Lt Knight, immediately after a quickie during which she stood against the wall in a dark corridor near the engine room, let her one-piece fall to her knees and took a quaking John Knight standing up, something which caused Knight's wilted banana to pulse with eagerness.

'Have you talked to Boots lately?' Ellie asked, smiling her happy smile as she cleaned herself on John's handkerchief.

'Of course,' Knight said, glad that his chore was over.

He was beginning to feel like a service stud and he was sure that Ellie was oversexed, so great were her demands on him.

'Have you noticed any difference in her?'

'No.' He wasn't really interested. He wanted only to get his handkerchief clean. He held it by one corner and turned his head away from the starchy smell of his semen on it. Why the hell, he was thinking, do all broads feel that a fellow has to furnish them a handkerchief? He'd lost more handkerchiefs that way. It didn't really matter back on Earth, where handkerchiefs were a credit a dozen, but out here he couldn't replace them and every time he whanged Ellie he had to smuggle a reeking handkerchief back to his quarters and run it through the dry-washer.

'And I thought you were the great white hunter,' Ellie said. 'Can't you tell when a girl is ready?'

'Ready for what?' Knight asked, his interest aroused, the sticky handkerchief forgotten.

'Ready for freddy, stupid,' Ellie said. 'Look, I'll spell it out for you. The kid has had a hangup because her puss was too small and I've fixed it and now she's making it like two or three times a week in the R & R. I think a real bone might be the answer to all of it.'

Boing!

'Why, lover,' Ellie cooed, seizing the rampant hardness in soft fingers.

And, so help him, the erection he got thinking of fresh meat in the form of Lt Pastele was wasted in another knee-bending muscle-wrenching whack at the insatiable Lt Martin, standing with her bare back pressed against the cool metal wall as Knight did all the work. And then he had to put his stinger away sticky because his handkerchief was already messed up.

Knight started his campaign that very day. He pressed

64

Ellie for additional details and found out that it would be four days before the doctor could allow Boots to exercise her newly enlarged cooch. He, knowing how distant the blonde Lt Pastele had been in the past, thought he'd need four days to soften her up. Meanwhile, he noticed that bastard, Sgt Decker, hanging around Boots. That bastard, Sgt Decker, was using a different time scale. He had counted the day of the operation into the medofficer's two weeks and, as a result, his plans for the blonde lieutenant were one full day ahead of the plans of Lt Knight.

'Lieutenant, baby,' Blackie crooned at Boots, 'I got five bottles of the best saved up from my ration, baby, honey.'

'This is an informal ship,' the lieutenant answered properly, 'but not that informal, Sergeant.' However, she found that she had trouble keeping her eyes off the big bulge at the front of Sgt Decker's one-piece. She found that she couldn't keep from imagining how it would be with the sergeant, who wasn't a bad looking fellow at all, even if he was an enlisted man.

'I've managed to preserve a glass or two from my ration,' Lt. Knight told Boots, later that same day. 'I'd be very pleased if you'd join me for a bit of relaxation after your watch.'

Well, as far as the offer went, the sergeant certainly had one up on the lieutenant, offering five bottles and a glass or two respectively, but, after all, Boots was an officer and, therefore, could not even begin to think about having a drink with an enlisted man. Then, too, she wasn't much of a drinker. Most of her ration went to Lt Martin, which in turn went partly to Lt Knight.

The pert little body of Lt Pastele was not thinking about bubbly booze. Her pretty little nipples hardened at the thought of the 'relaxation' offered by Lt Knight and she

65

said, under her breath, 'Yes, yes, I said yes, I mean yes.'
Aloud she said, 'I dunno, John – '

Thus encouraged, that marking the first time she'd ever used his name, Knight smiled his best smile and said, 'I'll be here when you go off duty.'

So for the better part of two earthhours Lt Pastele stewed in her own juices, reached down to pull the sensible white service panties away from her happy valley because they were sticking in the gooey mess of her anticipation.

'Well,' she told herself, 'I can go and have a drink with him, because it is three full days before I can have – er – uh – sexual intercourse, even if I wanted to.'

Had Sgt Decker been able to read minds he would have cheered, for Lt Pastele was also counting the day of the operation as part of the two weeks of healing and rest prescribed by her doctor.

Blackie saw that bastard, Lt Knight, hanging around outside control when he went in to relieve Lt Pastele and he cursed the bastard's hide when he peeked out and saw the two of them swinging down the damned corridor toward Knight's quarters. Blackie stewed for almost an hour, his mind fevered by his evil visions of what was going on in that bastard, Knight's quarters. He considered spying on them with the shipscan system. However, if he had activated it from control, he would have started the warning system going and there would have been all hell to pay. So he stewed and fretted. Then, almost an hour after he'd watched the two officers go off down the corridor together, he made a desperate move.

'Cap'n,' he said, having called the quarters of Asa Smith, 'I wonder if you'd mind doing me a favor.'

'If it is possible, Sergeant,' the Captain said graciously.

'I gotta case of the runs, Sir. Could you come down and hold my watch down for a few minutes?'

'Certainly,' Asa Smith said, only too happy to cooperate with the enlisted man. After all, he ran a happy ship. 'But I advise a visit to the medroom, Sergeant. No excuse for having the runs in this environment. No bugs or anything. Must be mental.'

'Sure,' Blackie said. 'Yes, sir. I'll be glad to visit the medroom, Sir, but right now – if you'll hurry – '

He put on a good act, standing on first one foot then the other when the Captain came into control and then he bolted, giving a quick, sloppy salute, forgetting the enforced formality which usually went with a changing of the watch. He reached his room just in time to be roused to a frenzy of hate and disappointment which sent his body temperature up four degrees, set off an alarm in the quarters of Ellie Martin and, later, added credence to his tale of being ill.

8

Boots Pastele walked down the corridor with her insides quaking. John Knight put his hand on her elbow and it was a calorific stimulus which caused her teeth to chatter. For the first time in her life Boots was going into a situation with carnal intent aforethought. Forgotten, for the moment, was the fact that she was not to allow intercourse for another three days. Forgotten were all her neoreligious concepts of morality. All the sweet neuro-muscular tensions in her body told her she needed a man, that she needed John Knight and needed him quickly.

Knight's quarters were neatly kept. His bunk was made carefully and there was nothing out of place. Boots just stood inside the door, leaning against the wall for support, while she watched Knight bend down to take a bottle from a cabinet and pour two glasses.

'I'm so sorry I have no more,' Knight was saying, smiling at her, letting his eyes run up and down her body. She felt like ripping off her one-piece so his eyes could caress her breasts, lay heavily on her taut stomach, wash over her thighs. She melted and ran down into her panties and felt as if she might fall if she moved away from the supporting wall.

'I suppose I'm a glutton,' Knight said wryly. 'I'm usually a bottle ahead of my ration and I bum and borrow shamefully. Poor Ellie – ' He paused. No time to talk about other girls. Might spook her. Girls had this strange sense of pride. When you were with one of them, she wanted you to be incapable of thinking of another girl. But Boots was looking at him with those pale eyes, her

68

little mouth set in a dreamy smile. 'Poor Ellie contributes at least half of her ration to my insatiable appetite.'

'Ummmmm,' Boots said, thinking of something even more intoxicating which Ellie contributed to John's insatiable appetite. She accepted the glass, downed the contents at a gulp and handed it back.

'My, my,' John said, beginning to hope that he was right, that the dear girl was as hot as the exhaust on his proton engines.

As for Boots, if she could have stepped out of her skin and walked around in her bones and looked at herself with an impartial eye, she would have failed to recognize herself. She had thrust her pelvis forward. Knight could see, with an eye which was becoming more and more inflamed, the sweet little mound of her *mons veneris*. He could see the rounded bumps of her breasts, tipped with little daggers which pushed against the silken material of her one-piece.

Boots purred deep in her throat. She'd never felt as she was feeling. She'd never, never felt so totally abandoned, so willfully wanton, so lewdly lascivious, so lastingly licentious, so voluptuously, deliciously ready for freddy. The psychdoctor, Ellie Martin, would have been able to analyze Boots at that moment. Ellie, with her knowledge, would have explained that the over-response to a look from John Knight was the result of pent-up frustrations, an accumulation of years which was released in Boots' subconscious mind by the minor surgery which made her a full-fledged woman for the first time in her life. Ellie would have pointed out, from first-hand knowledge, that Boots was a basically sexy girl who had bottled up her natural impulse in somewhat of a mixed morality and guilt complex for too many years and her behavior with John Knight was a logical result.

Without the medical terminology, Boots was hot as a

pistol. She kept forming those unspoken thoughts in her mind as John Knight sipped his liquor ration and looked at her with half-closed, sexy eyes. She wanted to yell, 'Dork me, daddy.' She looked at him and felt her cunny clutch at itself emptily and she wanted to scream at him, 'Gimme that yang-yang. Throw the organ to me, Morgan. I long for Long John. I cream for that crease cutter. I crave that cock.' And other associated terms which would have surprised Boots no end if she had been aware of her unbridled use of vulgar slang, even in her extreme need.

'Ah, Boots, honey,' Knight began tentatively, taking a step toward her.

'Yes I said yes I will yes,' Boots gushed, falling into his arms with a force which almost sent him tumbling backwards, and did send his glass – service plastic, fortunately – bouncing out of his hands to ping against the metal floor. 'Yes, baby, yes, whoooo, yes,' she said, the words muffled as she took his mouth in hers, enclosing the lips, all male and surprised, her heart going like crazy, in her fine, soft lips and licking his mouth with the flat of her tongue while her hands went down to grapple with penis erectus, an almost immediate condition of Knight's body. She felt the old thing through his one-piece and started fighting his zipper with shaking hands while she felt his tongue begin to respond to hers.

'Ah,' John Knight said, 'Boots, baby, you – uh, well as a matter of fact, Boots, honey, you – ugh – have the hairs on my chest caught in my – ha ha – in my zipper.'

'Oh, darling, sweetie, honey, don't kid around. Pole me with that poontanger. Give the goober to me, Groover.'

'Well,' Knight said, gritting his teeth and yanking on the front of his one-piece. The tangle of hair caught in his zipper, ripped out and he yelled, 'Ouuuuuuuch.'

'Oooooo, did I hurt ums, wittle baby?' Boots said,

lapsing into baby talk as she zipped the one-piece and followed it down, her wet tongue plowing a sensuous furrow along Knight's chest, his slightly softening gut and wrapping around the bald head of his butcher knife. 'Kiss to make umms well,' she mumbled, taking the firesnake into the soft tube of her mouth and sucking like a hungry baby.

It was his denuded chest which hurt, but she made it well quickly. He leaned back, jutted his probe out to make it easier for her, looked down on her bobbing blonde curls and moaned lustily. Then she was up, trying to swallow his mouth again, jerking off her one-piece to bare a lot of Boots, except that which was covered by the sensible service panties.

'Perhaps,' Knight said, 'we might be more comfortable – ' He indicated the cot and she threw herself down on it, let her lovely, soft white thighs spread. The panties stretched over the flat plane of her pelvic saddle, little spots of wetness showing through. Knight went to her, wrapped her in his arms and did some inspired work with his lips on her mouth, her neck, her coral tipped headlights.

'Oooo, John,' she whispered, 'ah, John, wow, yes I said yes I will yes and like that.'

He leaned on one elbow and looked at her. 'I get the idea, lady,' he said. 'You're willing. Well, my God, so am I. But I seem to remember that you're under doctor's orders to, uh, to well, you know what I mean.'

'Oh, hell,' she said, remembering. Three days to go. Three unholy days and her body was screaming, her entire being was transported to an extravagance of passion the like of which she'd never known. 'Well, there's no reason why we can't – ' She didn't put it into words. She pushed John onto his back and leaned over him, pushing first one melon and then the other into his mouth. Then

71

she went around the world, taking in each little area, giving Knight the greatest thrill he'd ever known until she ended up down there, making like a milking machine with her mouth. At one dear little moment she tried to punch the ripe, ruby-tipped nipple of one chi-chi into the eye of his tool and it wouldn't be fitted in, naturally, but then she put a hand on either side of her breasts and squeezed it between the soft mounds and Knight felt like he was going to come off and blow a hole in the underside of her chin.

She twisted, moaning her frustrations, sat on his face and he worked his mouth into the soft, wet, hot, musky woman flesh and tickled her clit with his upper lip until she was squirming and moaning with pleasure.

Suddenly, she came off it, threw herself down on him, seized the old prong with a shaking hand and tried to stuff herself with it. He, ever noble, remembered and twisted away, saying, 'No, we mustn't, darling. Not yet.'

'Oh, shit,' she said. 'I don't care. I gotta have it, baby. I *need* it.'

'Ah,' Knight said, moving slowly, lifting her, positioning her properly as inspiration flashed through his fevered mind. 'There might be a way, if ah, you are willing.'

'Oh, jeeese, willing? I'm steaming. Throw it to me, big daddy.'

'It might hurt a bit, at first,' he whispered, looking down on the twin globes of her posterior as she half knelt before him, breasts hanging prettily down underneath her.

'Arrrrrh,' she said.

It hurt a little at first. His hands went around her, found her creamy slit and began to manipulate *labia* and clit and it hurt like hell, but he was slow and easy, taking maybe five minutes to get it all in and by the time he got it in she was squirming and arching her rump asking for more and he, coming into the back door of love, felt her velvet soft and tight, like a soft glove, milking him down as she moaned and bucked and his hand stimulated her up front until, as he pumped fire into her vitals she climaxed roaringly, snuffling and snorting and moaning and wiggling and the squeezings of her soft rear were so powerful that Knight winced in agony-ecstasy.

And it was at this moment that Blackie Decker made it to his quarters and turned on the shipscan and tuned it to spy into the quarters of that bastard, Knight. He tuned in just in time to hear Boots cry out in a small voice, 'Ooops, whee, here I go, oh God!' He tuned in just in time to see that bastard, Knight, climbing that soft little bit of blonde fluff from the rear, like a goddamned dog, and he almost went ape. He almost ran to the armory and got a blaster to blast that bastard, Knight, but he saw, by using the movable lens of the shipscan and by going into short close-up, that that bastard, Knight, wasn't after all, jumping the gun on the doctor's orders. That bastard, Knight, was a perverted s.o.b. And that bitch, Pastele, was loving it, but the realization that Pastele was opening another avenue to Priapus, another one other than the one in which Blackie was interested, cooled him somewhat. He still steamed. He steamed enough to get out an Instaflex and take a dozen or more shots right off the shipscan screen, close up shots of that bastard, Knight, buggering that bitch, Pastele, against all regulations.

When it was all over and that bastard Knight, was alone in his room, and Pastele had staggered weakly back to her own quarters, Blackie thought it over and decided that it was for the best, after all. He had some damned incriminating evidence in the form of some Instaflex prints, blown up to 16 by 20 size in full color. You could even see the flush of passion in Pastele's pale face as she looked back over her shoulder and smiled at the pumpings of that bastard, Knight.

So Blackie bided his time. On F-Day minus one, he caught Knight and Martin in a clinch and got some good Instaflex shots of Martin going down on Knight to get him up so that he could put her down on the radiation suits there in the power room alcove. He shot a full dozen shots of various forms of action and then he had enough material to have all of them – that bastard Knight and both the officer bitches – in his power.

9

Lt Pastele walked strangely for a couple of days and admitted to Lt Martin that she was still a bit sore. Lt Martin, ignorant of the backdoor scene between Knight and Pastele, thought that maybe the small operation was taking longer than usual to heal and insisted on a viewing of the affected area. She pronounced the healing almost totally complete and said, again, that the original two week estimate of total time of incapacitation was correct.

Lt Pastele made a date with Lt Knight, because she was not fully satisfied by the rather unusual previous date with him, for the day which ended the two weeks.

Boots lay awake at times thinking of how it would be on that day. And when the day arrived, she couldn't sleep the previous night for thinking of it. It was pleasurable enough to have him coming in the back door and stimulating her with his hand up front, how would it be when it was the real, chockfull thing? She shuddered with pleasant anticipation.

She arose that day, did her morning watch, and went looking for Knight.

Knight, however, was counting time as Lt Martin counted it starting the day after the operation. He was saving his energy, hiding out from Lt Martin, who had given indications of being horny, in order to preserve his passions for the big day with Lt Pastele. So, not only was Lt Martin unable to find Lt Knight, so was Lt Pastele, who was ready, man, unable to find him.

And then she made the mistake of wandering into the territory of the enlisted man, Sgt Blackie Decker. Blackie was lying in wait for her. He popped out of his room and blocked her passage down the narrow corridor.

'Well, hello, Lt Baby,' he said, smiling a not unhandsome smile.

'Good morning, Sergeant,' Boots said, in good service form. 'Have you seen Lt Knight?'

'Naw,' Blackie said, 'I ain't seen the bas – I mean, No I ain't seen him, Sir.' He grinned to hide his anger at the mention of that bastard's name. 'But I got six bottles of bubbly saved up, Lt Baby, and I'm just aching to have some company.'

'I think you'd better get out of my way, Sergeant,' Boots said imperiously, pushing forward until her outriders pushed pointed and hard-soft into Blackie's chest, causing his eyes to pop a bit and not forcing him to move, not an inch.

In fact, he leaned toward her and whispered, 'Just one little drink, Lt Baby.'

But she pulled away, for she felt her boobs pushed against his hard chest and the nipples hardening. After all, she was primed to be loved and that bastard, Knight, was nowhere to be found. It wasn't right for him to disappoint her so. Not when she'd been on edge for weeks waiting for this day.

'Maybe just a little drinkie, Sgt Decker,' she agreed.

It took Decker five minutes to deck her.

Decker's quarters were larger than those of that bastard Knight. Decker, being a techman, had added little luxuries here and there. At first, it seemed unfair to Lt Pastele that a lowly enlisted man should have a larger Tri-vee screen and a refrigerator. And she wondered who inspected the E M quarters, for Sgt Decker had full-size dolls on the wall. He had three dimensional reproductions of such famous stars as Lana Lizabeth, all of them dressed in not enough fabric to clothe the cooch of one of them.

However, the officer had little time for wondering about the inequalities of life between those of high rank and enlisted men. For there was one horny enlisted man seemingly determined to get into her pants before she could decide whether or not she could forget the code of the service long enough to satisfy the itch in her bod.

Blackie, at thirty-eight, was a compact, small, barrel-chested man with straight, black hair and a set of dark brown eyes which seemed to be able to probe underneath the silken material of Boots' one-piece. He had a nice smile on a face which, when he was younger, had been termed a baby face but which, with time, took on an almost glum look of maturity. He kept himself in shape with isometrics and muscle-building pills, service supplied. His gut was hard as a rock and his legs were muscled and rounded to the point where one enamored broad, one time, told him that he had the most beautiful set of legs ever seen on a man. At the time, he didn't know whether to laugh or slug the wench, but finally decided it was a compliment, that she wasn't queer for legs or something, and began to be proud of his legs.

When Blackie smiled at a broad the broad knew she'd been smiled at and his smile, in his face which went handsome upon smiling, rather than glum, made Lt Pastele become a bit weak in the dimpled knees.

'A little drinkie,' Blackie cooed, handing the blonde officer the first properly chilled drink she'd had since embarking from Earth.

And it was Captain's stuff, not the medium-grade hootch which was standard issue. She took an appreciative swallow and smiled back at Blackie and looked around at the little luxuries. 'How do I get to be an enlisted man, Sergeant?' she said. 'You seem to do very well by yourself.'

Blackie shrugged. 'Well, the Cap'n's a non-drinker, so I can't see letting his ration just go to waste.'

So, she thought, it really was Captain's booze. The bastard was stealing it. Good, though. 'You, er, do you ask the Captain for it?'

'Are you kiddin'?' He made a quick move which forced Lt Pastele back into the bunk area to avoid being pressed immediately to his chest. 'Have a seat, Lt honey,' he whispered, forcing her back, back, until she was forced to sit to keep from falling backward onto the bunk. He sat beside her, refilled her service plastic glass and kissed her hand. He did it nicely. He picked it up in his and opened it up gently and pressed his lips into her palm. She felt a little thrill of awareness go through her and made no attempt to remove her hand from his possession as he touched his dry lips tightly to her knuckles.

'You have a nice hand, Lt sweetie,' he said, looking up into her pale eyes.

'I really must be going,' she said.

'Not a chance,' he told her.

'I have enjoyed the drinkie,' she said, very prim, very proper. She stood. He was sitting on the bunk. He was looking up at her with a smug grin on his face. 'But now I'd better get back, ha ha, to officer's country, before I'm missed.'

'Who'll miss you?' Blackie asked.

'Well, er – '

'That bastard, Knight?'

'Now, Sergeant,' she said severely. 'You must not speak of a superior – '

'Aw, balls,' Blackie said. He reached out and caught her by the cooch. His hand went under her mound, as she was standing slightly spread-legged, cupped her and lifted. She felt the heel of his hand press knowingly against her clit.

78

'Sergeant Decker!' she gasped, trying to get away. He rose, kept his hand between her legs, lifting her off the floor, feet dangling, balanced on his hand. 'Sergeant Decker! I'll report you to the Captain. I'll – '

'You'll have a ball, baby,' Blackie said, putting his other hand down the neck of her one-piece to close eager fingers over one of her hard-tipped headlights. He pinched a sweet nipple between his thumb and forefinger and she gasped and hit him in the face with her hand. Not hard. She didn't have the strength to hit him hard.

'This – is – conduct – unbecoming – an – officer,' she gasped, struggling to get her toes back onto the floor, instead of balancing on Blackie's hand.

'I'll be coming,' black-hearted Blackie said, 'as soon as I get this bedamned thing off you.' He was trying to hold onto the lieutenant's cooch, her headlight and work the zipper of her one-piece with his teeth.

'That will be all, Sergeant,' Boots said, moving her gluteal muscles, making her pelvis shift back and forth on Blackie's hand so that the heel of his palm would push against her swollen clit.

'Not by your G I drawers,' Blackie hissed, chipping the point of his front tooth, but bringing the zipper down far enough to expose the unbraed wonders of the prow of Lt Boots Pastele. And when he managed to capture one of the swinging beauties and grind the swollen little nipple between his teeth, rubbing it the while with his swollen tongue, the battle was over.

'I – must – go – now,' she said, riding his hard hand for all she was worth

'Not like that,' Blackie said. He picked her up and moved her over the bunk and dropped her. She landed on her back, like a cat seeking its feet, and Blackie had stripped out of his service one-piece before she stopped

79

bouncing on the springs, which were much bouncier than the springs on the bunks in officer country.

He looked huge. He looked like a little man with a telephone pole sticking out of his middle. He looked good enough to eat. He looked –

'I will not allow such familiarity,' she said sternly, trying to sit up.

'You want maybe I should throw it to you with my clothes on?' he asked, positioning himself over her, one knee forcing its way between her resisting thighs.

'I want you – to let me up,' she said. 'If you don't, I'll scream.'

'Fat lotta good that'll do,' Blackie said, pulling her one-piece down so that her arms were trapped by her sides, bending down to nibble happily at her exposed chi-chis. 'No one'll hear.'

'I'll report you,' she said, not really meaning it, but forced by the officer's code to protest. 'I've – I've never done anything like this and I – '

'Sure,' Blackie said, 'surrrrrre, baby, I know.'

'I mean, really. I've never, never – '

'What were you and that bastard, Knight, doing down in his hootch the other day?'

'I beg your pardon!' In trying to draw her shoulders up proudly, she pushed her left titty, the sensitive one, deeper into Blackie's sucking mouth and the feeling was so good it brought a faint little 'ooooooooooo' from her lips. 'I've never, never, never – '

'Ah, hell,' Blackie said, around a swollen nipple. 'What you call this?' He had put the Instaflex shots nearby, just in case a bit of blackmail was necessary.

He put them into her hands, letting the one-piece fall down off her arms and bundle around her waist. She saw herself, impaled from the rear by a grinning Lt Knight.

'How did you get these?' she squeaked, looking at the series quickly, struck most by the one which had caught her at the moment of terribly good climax. 'How – how – '

'You gonna scream?' Blackie asked. 'You gonna report me to the Captain? How'd you like it if I sent the Captain a set of those babies?'

'You wouldn't!'

'Not if you'll climb out of those clothes, Lt Baby.'

'It's blackmail, then,' she said.

'If it has to be.' He pulled the clothing down, exposed her mound, which was beginning to grow short hairs again, looking much like the cheek of a young boy with a three-week growth of beard. He used his finger knowingly, rubbing the pretty little clit gently. 'Does it have to be?'

'Well,' she said, grinning at him lewdly, 'as an officer I can't condone consorting with enlisted men, so it'll make me feel better if you, uh, *sort* of force me, like *sort* of blackmail me.'

He grinned back, pushing the one-piece away.

'Actually,' he said, 'you're so hot you're creaming your jeans.'

She pushed the sensible white service panties down by her knees, wiggled, kicked them away with such force that they flew across the room and lodged limply on the shade of the sergeant's reading lamp.

'Actually,' she said, making lewd, active, suggestive motions with her nubile body, 'I'm so hot I'm creaming my jeans.'

'Lord, Lord,' Blackie said, watching her hips rise and fall. 'You're a lot of girl, Lt Baby. You're a swingin' chick. I'd even go so far as to say you're goddamned beautiful.'

'Talk, talk, talk,' she said. 'Let's do it quick, then we can play.'

'OK,' he said. She drew her knees up slightly, showing him the lubricated *labia*, reaching for him with a grasping hand. He knelt between her outflung legs, felt her fingers close round his proddy readiness, leaned forward. He remembered, at the last minute, to be careful. She was loose and lubricated on the outside; he felt it when she pushed the nose cone of his massive missile into the softness, but he'd seen that tiny slit close up on the shipscan and he didn't want to spoil it with pain, not at this stage of the game. So he eased himself down. She wasn't the most experienced woman in the world, he decided. She was trying to insert him into the perineum. He shifted, felt the give, the hot, juicy feel of womanslit, stopped with the round head of his alter ego inside and asked, 'Hurt, Lt baby?'

'Arrrrrrg,' she moaned, launching herself up. She felt it penetrate then, quick and hard. She lunged again and he met her and she wished that Ellie had made it even bigger for she felt it slide and slide, going into her as if it would never stop and nary a twinge of pain, just good old gut thrilling sliding joy and she wanted to be filled with it, wanted it to go into her up to the very vitals and come out in her throat so that she could taste the goodness, too. 'Aww,aww,aww,' she cried, as Blackie hit bottom.

And Blackie wished that he had a tallywhacker ten feet long so that he could prolong that sliding bliss of entry. But it was good, even if it was only eight inches. She was all girl and he could feel the tightness. The medofficer hadn't ruined it, after all. It was tight and it chewed at him like a hungry calf as he probed it and pumped it and filled it and pulled out of it only to jump hard into it again and she was making loud little grunts of joy each time he hit bottom and thrilled her clit. Then, whoo, they both blasted off into a big jump and she was biting his lip and crying and laughing at the same time.

A very well-fucked smile on her face, she lay on an elbow and looked down into Blackie's face. He was on his back, wilted somewhat. 'I felt you,' she said, in an awed voice.

'I should hope so,' he said, fondly.

'I mean when you came off. I felt it gush out, gushing and spouting and all hot and funny.'

'Hummm,' Blackie said. 'Really?'

'Yes, really. I wanta feel it again.'

'Hummm,' he said.

'Please, Blackie,' she said.

He grinned. 'I cannot, as a responsible noncom, condone fraternization between the officers and the men.'

'Oh, Blackie.' She leaned into him, kissing his left ear.

'Besides,' he said, 'the flesh is weak.'

'What if I give you an order?' she said. 'What if I say, Sergeant Decker, I'm ordering you to make love to me?'

'You'd hafta talk to *him*,' Blackie said, flopping a limpness at her with one finger.

'Him,' she said, 'come to attention.'

Him didn't move. Blackie grinned. 'He can't hear you.'

'What if I got closer?' She bent over him, let her lips brush the smoothness. 'Attention, little space soldier,' she whispered. 'Can him hear me now?'

'Almost,' Blackie said. 'Almost.'

She took him into the softness of her sweet mouth. 'Ah,' Blackie said, 'he's listening. You have caught his attention.'

10

Six earthmonths is a long time to spend aboard a small ship with no swimming pool, and not even a shuffleboard court. The crew of the *Swinger* had spent six months on the way to J-day and only two of the ship's complement had found a way to fight the boredom of the day to day duty. It was a long six months and then there was the big J, which seemed to divide the trip into two distinct parts. The second six months, coasting down the deceleration hill from the space jump, two other members of the crew found that indoor games make days short and nights sweet.

Of course, all days were long to Capt. Asa Smith, who had only his love of duty, his devotion to the service and to his wife, Elenore. But, light-years away, his Elenore had discovered the joy of making meat sandwiches. In a playful mood one night, she picked up two members of a street gang, two strapping youths of eighteen who were dressed in skimpy scraps of black leather and denim with their muscles hanging out and the bulge of manhood very evident in their pouch-sacks of sequined leather. After a few spirited exchanges of wit like, 'You wanta get laid, lady?' she took them, the two young hoods, to her husband's luxurious apartment and made them a meat sandwich. She could feel their dorks deep in her, she being the meat in the sandwich, and could hardly breath with the delight of being punctured from both ends. She could feel the two huge whangs trying to push through the thin lining between her vaginal and anal canals and got quite a kick out of the homosexual delight of the two hoods, who said they could almost feel their hammers rubbing together, which made for a pretty sexy feeling, ending in a three-way circus of orgasm which left sweet Elenore pleasantly sated.

Light-years away, Capt. Asa Smith, true-blue and all-service, didn't even vent his natural passions on the innocent sensualizer. He merely let nature take her course and had to change his sheets quite a lot.

Meanwhile, Lt Ellie Martin was beginning to wonder if Lt John Knight was becoming impotent. He seemed to be losing all interest in the fine art of fornication and, more often than not, had to satisfy her with oral love, being unable to get it up. Since she was so directly involved, she did not analyze the situation, which actually, was easily seen. Knight had the hots for Lt Pastele, who after letting him dork her in the doughnut, seemed to lose all interest in him. He was, in his quaint state of Don Juanism, completely unable to get hot over the much used and over-familiar Lt Martin, lovely and eager though she was. He wanted Pastele and Pastele didn't give him a tumble.

Because Pastele had discovered that Sgt Blackie Decker was one hell of a fine lover, was tender and considerate and tough and passionate and loved their new discovery. They'd found out, that first night together in the sergeant's quarters, which were, really, much nicer than officer's country, that Lt Boots Pastele had a rare and exciting talent. She could use the *penis captivus* technique to perfection. At first, it was like a little spasm with an involuntary locking action of the muscles of her cush. Finding himself hung up like a dog, Sgt Decker yelped a bit, because he'd just brought both of them off with a roar, and then, the excitement of being actually imprisoned got to him and he fought against it so successfully that he brought them both off again and an exhausted Lt Pastele unlocked.

'Do that again,' Blackie said, the next time they were together. She tried. She couldn't, at first, then she discovered that by moving her navel six degrees to the left and an inch up she could lock the muscles, hold the good sergeant securely in place, squeezing him delightfully. Blackie, never having had a woman with a prehensile pussy, wasn't about to share his discovery with that bastard, Knight. So he kept his blonde baby happy with inventive sessions in his hootch and fed her Captain's booze and the days were happy ones for these two crew members, the same old slow days for the skipper and agony for Lt Knight, who wanted some of that Pastele so badly he was sneaking into the sensualizer to dream her up artificially.

Then, with only two more months ahead of them, Lt Martin who had been somewhat neglected of late, finally wised up and realized that the sergeant and Pastele were making it and that she wasn't. So she palled up with Sgt Decker and played on that age-old weakness of man, the natural urge of the male animal to screw all of them. He did. The variety was great. Ellie wasn't a talent like Boots where *penis captivus* was concerned, but she had a wild swing to her ass, making like a living corkscrew. Boots began to feel somewhat neglected, decided to try Lt Knight in the front door and did. After that it was a living ball for all of them, except that Knight resented having to share either of them with that bastard, Decker; and Decker hated like hell having to share his two lovelies with that bastard, Knight.

But the time was passing and the days, without the fine little indoor games, would have been long days. So the four of them lived by a philosophy of live and let live and the *Swinger* was one hell of a sexy ship until, three days before the final firing of the big proton engines to bring the ship down to cruising speed, Capt. Asa Smith decided to make an unannounced inspection tour of the ship. Sgt Decker had the watch in control, so it was not an invasion of Sgt Decker's privacy to enter the enlisted men's quarters. There, Capt. Smith found several empty bottles of Captain's rations, wine he was saving for a celebration party when the *Swinger* found a populated world, for Capt. Smith did not even anticipate failure. He would find people and people were people everywhere and people everywhere liked booze, so he'd been saving for a big bash with the beautiful people of Smith's World, for they'd surely name the newly discovered, populated planet after him. Now that bastard, Decker, had killed a good portion of it.

Furthermore, there was a pair of sensible, service panties hanging off the shade of Sgt Decker's reading lamp. Could it be, the Captain gasped, not really believing such a fantastic thing, that members of his crew were ignoring the service rules against copulating on government property? Could it be, perish the thought, that one of his officers was forgetting the service regulations against fraternization with the enlisted men?

In order to get to the bottom of things, Capt. Asa Smith moved quickly to the communications outlet in Sgt Decker's room, punched it up and was rewarded by a posterior view of Lt Boots Pastele riding Lt John Knight, straddling him with her knees under her, lifting her lovely body high and gasping with joy as she let the ship's artificial gravity pull her down to impaling goodness.

'My soul and body,' Capt. Asa Smith said.

'John, John, John,' Lt Pastele said, in increasing tempo timed with her up and down movements.

'My stars and garters,' Capt. Smith gasped.

'Go, gal,' Lt John Knight said breathlessly, taking his hands off Lt Boots Patele's boobs to use her hips as handles to drive her down harder into the mutual joy of total penetration.

'Oooooooeeeeeahhhhh,' Lt Pastele moaned.

'Arrrrg,' Lt Knight grunted.

The combat over, Knight and Pastele fell into each other's arms and relaxed. Capt. Smith, petrified by the enormity of it all, tried to figure out where he'd gone wrong. He stood in the sergeant's quarters, a handsome man in impeccable service blues, and couldn't believe that it could happen on his ship – two of his officers breaking every rule in the book. And, furthermore, that bastard, Sgt Decker, stealing his booze and having female service issue panties on his reading lamp, meaning only one of two things. Either Sgt Decker and one of his (gasp) officers were also screwing or Decker had a panty fetish. Either was bad, for a man in Decker's position could not afford to have his mind confused by either an illegal affair with a female officer or the twisted passions involved in a fetish. Decker, poor devil, had it tough, being the only enlisted man on board. Poor blighter hadn't, for example, had a meal with the other members of the crew since leaving Earth, for Capt. Smith ran a regulation ship and regulations said that officers' mess should be distinct and separate from the E M mess. But, Decker, being the only other person aboard with a working knowledge of the entire ship system – a good arms sergeant knew everything and Decker was one of the best arms and techmen the Captain had ever seen – was vital to the coming critical operations of the *Swinger*.

In three days they would begin the exploration of a new solar system. No one knew what was ahead. He'd need every man on board in tiptop shape and there was Decker, putting his inferior enlisted man's brain in a huge strain by worshiping a pair of officer's panties. Asa Smith had decided that no officer would stoop that low, stoop to getting into bed with an E M. And there were Pastele and Knight, lost in the evil throes of wicked passion, their alertness blighted by dissipation. That left him only one person on whom he could rely, the medofficer, Ellie Martin. He turned to go, to seek out the only other solid personality aboard, and his eye fell on a stack of Instaflex prints on a piece of furniture. There, on the top of the stack, was a shot of Lt Ellie Martin screwing Lt John Knight.

'My comets and suns,' Capt. Smith moaned, suddenly alone on the ship, the only sane man within millions of miles. They'd all gone crazy. To confirm it, he thumbed through Blackie's collection of Instaflex photos. Blackie had discovered that there was something deliciously lecherous about taking and looking at dirty pictures, and the Captain saw with popping eyes that the lowly enlisted man had used a self-timer to take pictures of Sgt Blackie Decker decking Lt Boots Pastele *and* Lt Ellie Martin. Then there were shots of Knight with Martin and Knight with Pastele and perversion crept in with a couple of shots of Pastele with Martin and it went on and on until the Captain's head was reeling.

Then the worst shock of all hit him. He looked over his shoulder and saw that, in the flesh on the viewscreen, Knight and Pastele were doing an inspired sixty-nine and it hit him that the only way he could be seeing that picture on the screen was through a complete invasion of the privacy of an individual, for the scene was definitely Lt Knight's quarters.

The shipscan system had been subverted!

He had to sit down. It was too much for him. Three days before the most critical portion of the voyage began and all his crew had gone animal on him!

Asa Smith was a different man when he walked back to his quarters. He looked in on Blackie, on watch, and saw that the sergeant was going through the motions of being alert. He didn't believe that the sergeant could be totally alert, not with the shameful things he'd been doing weighing on his mind. No one could pay strict attention to duty with the guilty knowledge of such crimes hanging on his head.

The question was what to do? He couldn't confine all of them to quarters. He had to have someone to help run the ship. He couldn't even call on his medofficer for help, for she was as depraved as any of them. He spent long hours in his quarters wondering what to do about the situation and decided, finally, to let it ride until they had finished the exploration of the solar system ahead. Then he would institute action. Back on Earth, he'd see them all court-martialed. The enlisted man would get twenty years at hard labor on the Mars mines and the officers would be severely reprimanded. And it would serve all of them right. John Knight wouldn't get his promotion to Space Captain and the females would be frozen in rank for the next twenty years. The service could not abide such conduct.

And if it was discovered that any of the officers had anything at all to do with the subversion of the shipscan – well, he just didn't know what would happen. It would be a scandal from which the service would be long in recovering.

During the three days before the final deceleration firing, Capt. Smith couldn't sleep. Every time he'd drop off he'd dream that the person on watch had left his position to go screw someone and the ship crashed head on into an asteroid. He would sneak from his quarters to check, find the person on watch doing his duty, sigh with relief, and begin to worry the minute he was back in his quarters again.

The entire crew was on duty when the big firing was

90

fired and it went off without a hitch. They thundered and shuddered down to cruising speed and got a good look at the planetary system ahead. The unimpressive little class C sun, so much like old Sol, back home, had a family of five. Of the five, two were close in, blasted by the fire of the solar furnace, and two were far out, frozen by the cruel cold of space. That left only one in the mid-range and Capt. Smith's heart sank. The planet was, according to the measurements of a surprisingly efficient Lt Pastele, approximately Earth size, but the Captain had hoped for at least two of the three larger planets to be in the habitable range of solar heat.

However, as the ship neared the third planet, there were encouraging signs. Pastele, laboring over her instruments, reported oxygen in the atmosphere of the third planet and Decker, off duty officially but standing watch on a huge electron telescope, yelped with delight and excitement and sent the entire complement of the *Swinger* into a state of near ecstasy.

'She's an oxygen planet, all right,' Decker was saying, in an undertone, with no one in particular listening. 'I see regular oceans and there's green to indicate vegetation and – ' He was silent, suddenly alert, leaning forward into the telescope. 'Captain!'

The tone of Decker's voice made Asa Smith turn, a quizzical look of anticipation, dread, or simple, sure alertness on his face.

'My God, Captain, I see it!'

'What is it, Sergeant?'

'There's a city down there!'

You could hear the quiet. No one breathed.

Down below the big proton engines hummed as they'd been humming for a year, earthtime, and the little servo-mechanisms purred and clicked. The five humans in the control room were frozen into silence, an awed silence.

91

Each had his own thoughts but there was this element in all of them – *we are not alone*.

'Are you sure, Sergeant?' the Captain asked, at last.

'Take a look, Sir. Down there. Quadrant A, upper grid. Between those two mountain ranges in the wide valley.' Blackie was standing beside the skipper as Smith bent and followed the instructions and saw what could be a city or a mass of rocks or –

'No lights,' Smith said.

'No radiation,' Lt Pastele reported, having zeroed in on the area indicated by Sgt Decker. 'If it's a town it's not on atomics.'

'It's a city,' Captain Smith said, his voice soft and pleased. 'My God, it's a city.' He looked into the scope for a long time, trying to hide the tears of joy which crept down his cheeks. Finally, he had to turn and he saw that the two female officers were also crying and that John Knight was blowing his nose on a handkerchief which looked frayed, as if it had gone through the dry-washer too many times.

'We'll go down,' the Captain said. 'Full alert. Sergeant, man your defense. Lt Pastele take the wheel. Knight, stand by to give me blast on an instant's notice. Martin, man the communications.'

It was a procedure which had been rehearsed many times. Each man fell into his job with long-practiced movements and the *Swinger* dropped its tail and went falling down into a rich atmosphere which became fully breathable at a few thousand feet. Down the blasting proton engine tubes roared a hurricane of force which stopped the little ship and let her hover over the city below while Lt Knight made every effort to establish some kind of communications with the people down there; he used every communications system known to man and got nothing in response.

Decker, on his defense post, having enough force at his fingertips to level the city below into a pool of molten metal, made vocal reports during the descent.

'They ain't no one down there,' he said, falling into old speech patterns in his amazement. 'It's empty!'

The city stretched below them, clearly visible to the naked eye now. It was a fine city, well planned. The buildings pointed up at them from a broad plain beside a river which meandered off into the distance. There were green areas throughout, as if the being who planned the city felt that it was important to break the hardness of artificial lines with nature's growth. Here and there small lakes dotted the city and a well defined network of streets indicated that the inhabitants used some form of ground transportation.

'It looks like Dallas,' Blackie said.

'Dallas doesn't have lakes,' Martin retorted.

'But it looks so homelike,' Pastele said.

'Definitely humanoid,' Asa Smith said. 'It was built by humanoids.' He had been scanning the deserted city and was genuinely puzzled. Were they all frightened by the appearance of the ship? Judging from the sophisticated structures below, by the huge network of streets and the radiating roads leading out of the city, the beings who built it were in an advanced state of technology. Surely the sight of one ship from space wouldn't panic an entire city. Unless – He leaped toward Sgt Decker's position. What if he'd blundered into a war? What if those people down below thought his ship was the enemy and, at that very moment, were training rockets, guns, weapons of which he had no knowledge on his *Swinger*?

'Report!' he barked at the arms sergeant.

'Nothing to report,' Blackie said.

'Missile activity?'

'Negative.'

93

'Aircraft?'

'Negative,' Blackie said, swinging his head with the search radar.

'Ground fire?'

'Negative.'

'I get a total negative on a body heat search, Sir,' Lt Martin reported.

Asa Smith began to feel slowly sick, wondering if he'd come all those light-years to find a dead city, a deserted planet. 'Take her down to five thousand,' he ordered.

At five thousand feet there was still no activity to be seen in the city below. Not at three thousand nor two thousand.

The ship from the Earth touched down in a park-like area in the center of the city. From a height, the park looked neat and well-kept. Close up it was scraggly. Grass was knee deep and bushes had grown over walkways.

Medofficer Martin began to check the atmosphere and reported it to be surprisingly near the composition of Earth atmosphere, so near that as she figured it, the crew could breathe it without artificial aids of any kind. Then she began a lengthy and careful check of airborne bacteria and discovered an almost total lack of contamination. She took samples, by remote, from nearby vegetation and, after twelve hours of continued testing, announced to the Captain and her crewmates that the world on which they had landed was apparently free from any sort of harmful germ or virus, that the air was very sweet and that, pending a few final tests, they could all venture forth.

The final test involved a few friendly, well fed animals of the rodent family, animals who had been kept suspended in inactivity throughout the long voyage out. Revived, the furry little beasts were sent out into the atmosphere remotely, and they were left there while the *Swinger* slumbered through a night of approximately the same length as an earthnight. The medofficer checked them first thing in the morning and found them to be healthy. The little beasts were so healthy, in fact, that she snickered and called Lt Pastele to the view port to see.

'Why the little beggars,' Boots said, giggling.

The little beggars were fornicating with a vigor which brought more giggles, drawing the attention of the male members of the *Swinger*'s crew. Even the dour Capt. Smith smiled as he saw the two tiny beasts finish a set, rest, with their little sides moving in and out with their panting, and leap back into the fray to copulate with jerky, swift movements.

'I'd say, Lt Martin,' Asa Smith said, 'that the air out there is very healthy.'

'That's my report, Sir. I recommend that we send out an exploration party at the Captain's convenience.'

'Thank you, Lieutenant,' Smith said formally. 'I will be taking a party out myself, if you'll be so kind as to help prepare the equipment.'

'You, Sir?' John Knight asked.

'Me,' Capt. Smith said, determined that he was to be the first to set foot on Smith's Planet, as he was already calling it in his mind.

'Well, then, I'll go along,' Knight said.

'I'm sorry, John,' Smith told him. 'As second senior aboard, you'll have to remain here. I'll take Sgt Decker with me.'

'But, Sir – ' Knight protested.

'You'll all have your chance,' Asa Smith said. 'However, as your Captain, I feel it my duty to go first, to explore the possibilities of danger.'

'Yes, Sir,' Knight said.

Blackie Decker made a wry face. He didn't mind the Captain going first to explore for danger, but he wasn't wild about going with him.

11

Upon closer inspection, the city showed its age like a bepainted woman who, as the evening wears on, soaks up her make-up and shows wrinkles through. The park-like area in which the *Swinger* had landed gave way to open streets of cracked cement – or a cement-like substance. The dust of age swirled around the feet of the two men as they left the area of vegetation and stepped onto the street.

The buildings, built of stone and metal, seemed to be intact, but bare looking, since all non-permanent materials had long since rotted away.

Smith led the way. Blackie, carrying a deadly blaster, walked two paces to the rear, looking around nervously, ready to demolish anything that moved. The street was much like any Earth street, except for the fact that it was dead, undeniably dead. Asa Smith could look at the street, at the bare, empty buildings and feel in his bones that he was the first living thing to walk that street for centuries.

'Right spooky, huh, Captain?' Blackie said, coming up even with Smith but continuing his vigilance.

'I don't think you're going to see anything to shoot with that weapon, Sergeant,' Smith said.

They rounded a corner and entered a public square. Ahead of them a statue stood, stark against the sky. With a pounding heart, Asa Smith hurried his steps and looked up at the thing of stone. The being represented was a man, definitely a man. He had a hawk nose and a strong chin and he stood with a very military stance, his hand on the hilt of a sword-like weapon.

'Like us,' Blackie said. 'They were just like us.' He put one hand on the base of the statue and looked up into the face of the man who was immortalized in the stone. 'Wonder what happened, Sir.'

Asa Smith couldn't answer. All this way. All this way to find a world with people just like Earth people and they were gone, dead, dead and gone. He felt like crying. He felt like yelling up at the blue, cloud-spotted sky to ask why?

'Shall we take a look inside one of these buildings?' Blackie asked, after they'd walked perhaps a half-mile down a dead street with the age-old dust making little puffs around their feet. The Captain nodded affirmation and Blackie, blaster at the ready, led the way into an entrance which was lined with a beautiful, marble-like material which looked as if it were part of a very functional, very much alive building. However, inside, the floor was exposed down to metal joists and, here and there a weed, looking pale from lack of direct sunlight, poked its head up from an accumulation of dirt. The structure had been built of durable metals and stone, save for floor coverings and decorative pieces and it had weathered and decayed down to the permanent materials. It had been a long, long time since anyone or anything human walked in that building.

And it was like that everywhere Blackie and the Captain went in that dead city. They spent two hours looking for signs of life. They found some more evidence that the race which had once inhabited the city was humanoid, in the form of small statuary and in some metallic printing plates in what was, obviously, a newspaper office.

Greatly saddened, Smith gave the order to return to the ship. He carried a little statuette, a representation of

97

a very Earth-like girl with large breasts and beautiful body and little eyes with a tiny slant. They were admitted to *Swinger* by Knight, who had been on guard.

'Any sign of them, Sir?' Knight asked. Looking at him, Asa Smith was reminded of the lieutenant's depravity, but the man was, Smith thought, keeping up appearances.

'Nothing,' Smith said.

'I think you'll be interested in visiting the medroom, Captain,' Knight said.

'Oh?'

'The test animals are dead.'

Smith felt a sudden contraction in the small of his back. He was standing in the port of the *Swinger*. Involuntarily, he looked back over his shoulder into the dead city. He off-loaded his equipment, handed it to Sergeant Decker and hurried to the medroom, where Lt Martin, assisted by Lt Pastele, had just completed an exhaustive autopsy.

'What is it, Lieutenant?' the Captain asked, his face calm, strong.

'As far as I can make out, Sir,' Ellie Martin said, unsmilingly, 'they fucked themselves to death.'

'Lieutenant!' Smith said. 'I remind you of your rank and of your position – '

'Begging your pardon, Sir, but that's just it. They died of exhaustion and dehydration and starvation brought on by the simple and obvious fact that they wouldn't stop fornication long enough to eat or drink or rest. I think it must have had something to do with the suspension during the trip out. Perhaps, and I really hesitate to analyze the emotions of small rodents, but perhaps they were in the act of breeding when they were suspended. You are aware, I'm sure, that suspension does not totally stop the mental process. A sort of dream-like consciousness exists and, perhaps, during that long year, the little beasts were

98

dreaming of their breeding and when we thawed them, well – '

'They – er – ah – copulated themselves to death,' Smith said, feeling a vast relief. He did not want to have to face something deadly on Smith's Planet. He wanted, if nothing else, to be able to report that he'd found a planet suitable for human migration. 'You're sure it's, ah, nothing in the air? No germ? No virus?'

'As near as I can make out, Sir,' Ellie said, 'and we've been at it since you left, there's not a living thing on this planet except a species of bee which is so harmless it doesn't even have a stinger. There's no bacteria except some harmless ones which promote decay. No house flies, no mosquitoes, no nothing. It's as if someone or something wiped out everything but the insect bacteria necessary to keep a growth of vegetation going.'

'Very strange,' Smith said, 'but let's withhold any final judgment until we've made a more thorough search.'

The *Swinger* cruised the atmosphere for seven days with every search instrument going, and added exactly nothing to the already discovered list of living things on Smith's Planet. Bees and bacteria necessary to the continuation of vegetation. That was it. Then the *Swinger* became a submarine and explored the seas of the planet and they were devoid of all life save the little microorganisms which convert water to oxygen and keep the atmosphere in balance.

In short, Smith's Planet was a paradise which contained all the necessary ingredients for human population, but none of the pests. Earth people could come to Smith's Planet and introduce only the beneficial species of animal life. The oceans could be populated with food fish without sharks or barracuda or Men-O-War and there would never be poison snakes or biting insects or, if proper care were taken, destructive germs.

Of course, there was a huge question to be answered. What had happened to the population of the planet? For there were more cities. There were cities on the seas and by the rivers and in the pleasant mountains. There were towns and villages in the wide, fertile plains and huge dams and works of engineering art to prove that the population of the world had been advanced in technology, though a bit behind Earth. There were flying machines and ground machines and strangest thing of all, there were no signs of violence. There were no bombed out cities. The aircraft were parked, decaying, on airfields. The ground cars were in shelters, rubber wheels rotted away. It was as if an entire world had gone to sleep and never waked.

Ellie was the one who first voiced the suspicion that the people of Smith's Planet had died in bed. Exploring what seemed to be a residential district, she found dental plates in the remains of what seemed to be a piece of sleeping furniture. Further examination of other houses revealed the same evidence. Items of jewelry, teeth-fillings and other nondecayable items were found in what all agreed were bedrooms.

Captain Asa Smith shuddered to think of billions of people dying in their beds. He found himself looking over his shoulder to seek out the cause of such a mass disaster. He took the *Swinger* to what seemed to be the world's most populous city or at least what *had* been the world's most populous city, put her down in an overgrown park and told his crew to find out all they could about the people of this world.

'We will maintain a reasonable security,' Capt. Smith told his people. 'However, in weeks of searching this planet we have found no living thing save a harmless species of bee, so we do not want to slow down our investigations with needless precautions. We will, of course, keep guard on the ship, but in order to speed our search for information, each of us will operate individually. We will search the libraries, the art centers, the shops. We will take back with us enough material to give the Earth's scholars a complete picture of the planet and its former people.'

'Fine,' Lt Martin said. 'There's a medical center here I want to examine.'

'I'll work in the library,' Lt Pastele said. 'Perhaps I can get a line on the language there.'

'Sgt Decker,' Smith said, 'you may take first watch on the ship.' He started buckling on equipment. 'I'm going to free-lance all over the city and just play hunches. Lt Knight, you may choose your area of investigation.'

'I thought I'd take in a few of the art galleries,' Knight said. 'I want to find a cutie like the one you brought back that first day out.'

Capt. Asa Smith frowned. It was like Knight to think of women, when all the women of this world had been dead so long that their very bones were dust, scattered dust. And, thus reminded, Smith felt once again his heavy responsibility. He had to punish his crew for their complete disregard of regulations during the trip out. They would not be allowed to conduct themselves so disgracefully on the way home and that meant that he would have to confront them with his evidence – that which he'd seen with his own eyes – at some early time. Not, however, before they'd done their jobs on Smith's Planet. He was not going to start a big thing about regulations until he had what he wanted in the way of information, books, art objects, scientific gadgets, aboard the *Swinger*. Perhaps, if her luck held, his ship would take back to Earth not only the knowledge of the first habitable planet to be discovered, but some great discovery which had been known to the people of Smith's Planet and was unknown on Earth. Perhaps –

Thus Capt. Asa Smith dreamed as he ventured forth alone, on Smith's Planet, a world he'd named for himself, a world on which life had ceased to exist centuries before.

All life, that is, save the Gant.

The Gant, vast appetites stirred by the brief fling with the two small animals of minimum intelligence, had held itself in check for long days waiting, waiting, waiting. Days, however, were nothing to the Gant. Centuries had passed since life stirred on the world to please the Gant. And before that, before the people of what the new creatures called Smith's Planet ventured out to find their fate, it had been millenniums and before that –

Caution told the Gant to wait. Soon the creatures would fly back through a space which was impassable for the Gant – to a teeming world of billions and billions of living things. Soon the Gant could live again, gloriously, wonderfully, satisfyingly, gluttonously. However, it told itself, waiting there, watching the five new creatures, not so gluttonously as to depopulate the world, as had been done here, on what they called Smith's Planet. No. Never again.

Of course, it had been millenniums since the Gant had lived the tiniest orgasm when it came home to Smith's World that glorious day a few centuries back. The Gant had lost control. Now things would be different. Now the Gant would be careful, calculating, would save a scrap for the next millennium; for creatures of this type which were now spreading out from the little ship developed so slowly in the universe. The Gant would not lose control. Oh, there'd been the moment of gluttony with the two tiny little animals which the creatures had put out into the atmosphere. That was a fine little moment, but it had put some sense into the Gant's mind. If the Gant let itself go and lived the other five creatures aboard the ship, there'd be another long, long wait before they came again, so, the Gant would not – except, maybe – well, it might not hurt anything – Oh! Space! – it had to. Just a little bit. That one. Their leader. Bottled up inside were the most delicious frustrations. One of his year's worth of frustrations. The Gant had to. It couldn't help itself. It –

12

Capt. Asa Smith walked down the middle of a broad avenue. On all sides were the magnificent buildings of a past civilization. Above him, the sky was blue, dotted with fleecy, white clouds. The breeze was cool. He estimated it to be autumn of the year on Smith's Planet. He walked with the pride of knowing that he'd discovered it, this beautiful world, and this joy almost compensated for the fact that there was nothing left of the once huge population of the world. Perhaps something sinister had once stalked the people of the planet, but it, like the people, was long gone.

He reached a square, walked to look at the statue in its center. Another hero. Much like the hero of the first square he'd seen on his world. The people of his world must have been great for heroes, but then, weren't all humanoids? They like to exalt one of their own, thus lifting themselves a bit. Perhaps, and he boggled slightly at such immodesty, they'd build a statue to him one day. The man who found a place for expansion. After all the dead planets, all the unlivable planets, he'd found a paradise.

He walked. A little park, overgrown like the rest, drew his attention. He entered, pushing down a mostly over-grown pathway. Suddenly, he entered a small clearing. A little lake was in front of him and tall trees, very much like the pine trees of earth, shaded the banks of the lake. Their dark shadows had discouraged undergrowth so that the gladey spot of shade along the bank of the lake was clear, covered with a deep, soft, clean carpet of needles.

Smith sighed. He loosened his equipment belt, let the load sink down onto the carpet of needles and sat down. The breeze was pleasant. The sun filtered down here and there in a dreamlike beam. Something had attracted him to the spot and when he remembered, it was with a deep glow of pleasure. The little glade was much like the lakeside spot where he'd proposed to his Elenore on a bright earthday years ago when she was sweet and young and so desirable that just to look at her made his loins tighten. God, she was beautiful, all long legs and big bust and sweet body and smiling lips. Young, hot natured. He knew that for he'd held her in his arms and kissed her until their blood boiled together and he wanted to –

'Hello, Asa,' she said, sitting beside him in a long, flowing, old-fashioned thing which clung to her curves. She was young, smiling.

'Elenore!' He looked at her, mouth wide open in surprise.

'Yes, darling.'

'It can't.' He turned. He looked away. He shook his head and rubbed his eyes and looked back and she was still there and the loose dress had been pushed back to allow her to bathe her feet in the water. 'It can't be,' he said. 'I'm hallucinating.'

'I know it's difficult to believe, darling,' she said. 'But listen. I'm not light-years away. I'm here.'

'No,' Asa said. 'No.'

'It's very logical,' she said. 'The Muleholtzen labs labored busily a day and here I am, looking as if I were alive.' She reached for his arm and her hand was alive, hot, woman. 'Which I am, darling. I'm alive. It's called astral projection. It's a project financed by the service to build the morale of the troops. You just know the general

105

location of some traveling space hero, send a projection of his loved one and, presto, here I am.'

'No,' Asa Smith said, his senses stunned. 'And yet – ' Earth science was so terrifically advanced. They were always coming up with something. And, God knows, it was a wonderful idea. He'd suffered without her for a year, an eternal earthyear. 'You're not like the sensualizer,' he whispered, wanting to believe, 'you're not just in my mind?'

'I'm very real,' she whispered, taking his hand and putting it down the loose neck of her dress until it encountered soft breasts, hot and uncovered.

'But you're young. You're too young. I mean, we're not kids anymore, Elenore.'

'I know, isn't it wonderful? It's because a lot of the astral projection process depended on the picture you have in your mind of me. Your mind is the focal point, drawing me in after I'm projected from Earth and you still see me this way, darling, young and pretty. And I feel pretty and, God, Asa, I feel so hot. It's been a year, Asa. Don't make me wait another minute, please, darling.'

God, she was sweet, mouth-wet, hot, tasting of his favorite lipstick, her body molding to his in hunger, begging for him, her breasts under his hands.

'Take it off, darling, rip it away, now!'

And it gave easily. The blowing material ripped and fell and she was exposed to him, white, lying on the brown, soft needles, body writhing in his caress.

'Your clothing, Asa,' she whispered around his lips. 'Oh, quickly!' And he denuded himself and she was there waiting for him as he knelt between her long, white, hot legs. He pushed her thighs apart so that he could see the dark flower of her woman-parts, see the soft *labia* and the little iris-rose of flesh which was the opening to her vagina as he parted the *labia* with shaking fingers and aimed himself there. It was white-hot glory and he lunged, almost cruelly, deep into her depths. She moaned with her lush joy as he filled her, as they reached climax almost immediately and lay there in each other's arms whispering about how wonderful it was.

'I love you so much, Elenore,' he told her. 'God, I wish there were two of you so that I could love you more.'

It was almost too much. For, no sooner had he wished his wish than she was two, alike, lovely, one holding his partially deflated penis in her used, lubricated woman-heat, the other kissing his left ear and pushing her hot breasts against his shoulder, rubbing her wet-hot woman-hood against his muscular thigh.

'Gaaaa,' he said, frightened.

'No, darling,' she whispered, the original one.

'It is I,' the second one said. 'It's a part of the astral projection phenomenon.'

'It's your mind,' the first one said.

'Like the sensualizer,' Asa said, feeling belittled.

He'd been making love to a figment of his imagination.

'No, not like that at all,' the first one said. 'I'm real. She's real and she's me and you can have me anyway, anytime in time, darling. And I'll leave you this – ' She put a ring into his hands, the ring she'd worn since that day beside the lake. ' – to prove that I'm real. Would it be real, the ring, if I weren't? You can keep it and know that I was really here.'

'And in the meantime,' number two said, 'you can have something no other man has ever had. You can have your wife in multiples of herself, darling.'

It was a problem in morals. First, Asa Smith slipped the ring onto his little finger. Then he looked at his wife, both of her. Muleholtzen's lab had done some wonderful things, but creating two of his Elenore was by far the most wonderful. He accepted it. He accepted it as his due and he slipped away from number one and put it in number two and her vagina was fresh and tight and not used and the contrast was wonderful. Number one put a soft hand on the base of his penis where it was entering number two and played with his pendant testes and having two of his Elenore was so wild he wished he had three and, lo! there were three, number three spread out on her back beside the penetrated number two, legs open so that by bending his neck Asa Smith could sip the nectar from the bedewed *labia* of her dark flower. It went on and on until he came with thunderous passion and number two came with him and number three, with his tongue working furiously, came with both of them and number one, who had had hers, laughed and pushed a lubricated finger up his anus and tickled his throbbing prostate gland into pumping even more hot semen into the pulsing vagina of number two.

Alone with Elenore number one, grown into an adult, mature Elenore to match her current image in his manly mind, he talked and talked and she lay nude by his side until, later, he wanted her again, wanted her as he'd never wanted her before. There was something in him which drove him to take her and he rolled atop her to find her willing. He'd never been a multiple threat before. Perhaps it was the year of denying himself. The day passed in lovely fornication. Late in the evening, tired, happy, drained, Capt. Asa Smith knew it would soon be time to say good-bye. But it wasn't to be as long a good-bye as the last one. For now the Astral Projection project would send her to him when he needed her.

'Kiss me before you go,' Elenore said.

He kissed her, tenderly, lovingly.

'Once more?' She was woman, eternal, teasing, lubricous, well-used woman asking for more love.

He laughed. 'God, baby, I'm killed.'

'I'll bet I can make you want to.'

'More power to you, darling, but I doubt it.'

'Watch me, Asa.'

Before his eyes she grew younger. From his mature Elenore she grew younger through her twenties, into her teens, became a leggy, full-blown sixteen year old, the way he'd never seen her, since he had met her when she was past twenty.

'God, you were beautiful,' he whispered.

'I'm virgin.'

He felt a glow. Then, as the glow grew and became a hardness where he had thought there was nothing left, she grew younger. Her full breasts grew harder and smaller until she was a skinny fourteen year old with budding breasts and a lovely little body with a tiny waist and a little bush of woman hair which looked out of place on her small body.

'You can have me, darling,' she whispered, in a young voice. 'You can have me like this if you want me.'

'But – ' He wanted to say it was perverted. She was just a child, just a skinny, beautiful little child.

'It's all right. It's me. I love you. Take me, darling.' The skinny, beautiful little body came to him, let him wrap his arms around it. He felt his hugeness pressed against her hard little stomach and she put her hand down on it and shuddered. 'Do me, darling, now!'

He was still reluctant. To assist him in making up his mind, she lay back on the soft carpet and spread her legs. She put her hands down, pulled the *labia* apart, showed him the tiny opening. 'Now, darling,' she said, heat in her voice.

Over the pounding of his heart he could hear her breathing – gusty, then sighing. He bent, kissed the virgin spot. One of his lifelong regrets had been the fact that

109

Elenore had not been virgin when they married. She'd had a love affair with a space marine at the age of eighteen, she'd told him. Now, thanks to Muleholtzen's heirs, he was being given a second chance.

'Don't let me hurt you, darling,' he whispered. 'Please tell me if I'm hurting.'

'I don't care,' she gasped. 'I don't care. I want you so badly.'

He felt her fingers close around his hardness. He felt the glans penis pressed into the hot little opening and she began to move up against it. He felt the heat and the moistness and he moved in and she winced and moaned. But she was so hot! She lunged up and he felt a tight squeeze as his penis entered and the tightness was delicious! He felt the spasms of joy in her softness as he fullfucked her, throwing it in deep, deep, her pain gone and her little girl's body wiggling in his lustful embrace and when he went it was the most joyful orgasm he'd ever known.

When she was gone, he was finally devastated. He wept. He was weak, tired. He pulled his clothing on, carried his equipment, walked slowly and sadly back to the *Swinger*. He found Sgt Decker sleeping a sleep of exhaustion in the grass beside the entrance hatch.

13

When the Captain and the other officers left Blackie aboard the *Swinger*, he made his rounds, checking on all equipment. He didn't mind staying on board. He'd seen all there was to see out there. It was a dead world. What he wanted was a live piece. In the excitement of exploring the new planet, the girls had been so busy, and the Captain had been so everywhere present, that he'd gone a week or more without a piece of whang and, having been spoiled by the willingness of Boots and Ellie in the past six months, he felt put upon.

After he'd made the rounds and found all systems working like they should work, he found time hanging heavily on his hands. He decided there'd be nothing wrong with stepping outside for a breath of air. The others had been gone for a couple of hours.

He saw the movement before the person was near enough to be identified and thought it was one of the officers coming back. He leaned against the ship and waited and then he was standing upright, tense, his hand on the butt of the blaster strapped to his waist.

'Halt and be identified,' he yelled, because the person approaching was not the Captain, not Knight, not Pastele or Martin. The person approaching was a woman dressed in a cute little short skirt affair with her tits bare as a buck and the nipples painted silver. 'Whoa,' Blackie yelled, as she came closer.

'I come as a friend,' she said.

'How come you talk Earth?' Blackie asked, his eyes popping at the size of those knockers.

'Through your mind,' she said.

'Oh yeah?' He was having frightening thoughts of mind-domination and stuff like that. 'What am I thinking now?'

'You like my – uh – knockers.'

'Yeah?'

'And you *want* me to be a friend.'

'Hell yes,' Blackie said. 'We been looking all over for you people.'

'There are only a few of us left.'

'Yeah, well, what happened to you?'

'It was a thing from space,' the girl said. Blackie was examining her with great curiosity. She looked to be young, say about twenty. She was built like a ship of the line, solid and beautiful. Her skirt just barely covered her box and those knockers were something else. She had lips which just begged to be kissed and eyes sorta slanted, real sexy like.

'Not a thing, really, some sort of ray,' she went on. 'Suddenly, all of our men were sterile. There were no more births. Our population died of old age and – '

'Then how come you're so young?'

'I'm coming to that. Before the last of the scientists became too old, they took the last few girl babies born on the planet and put them into suspension.'

Blackie nodded. It was possible. They had the suspension process on Earth. It was against all laws to use it on human beings, but it was used on animals. They'd brought a couple of little animals with them in suspension, the two that fucked themselves to death – and what a way to go, man.

'There was an alert system which was designed to waken one of us when we were visited from space, as our scientists thought we would be. You see, we'd just developed the art of space travel when it happened.'

'So you're the only one woke up,' Blackie said.

112

'I have come to see if our genes are compatible,' the gorgeous girl said.

'Huh? What do you mean?'

'I mean, Sergeant, that I'd like for you to try to impregnate me.'

'Knock you up?' Blackie grinned. It just happened that he'd never been given that opportunity. As a service man with a good record, a healthy body and a brain which wasn't too well educated, except in tech matters, but which was a good brain, he was entitled to have two kids, but to have kids you had to be married.

'Yes,' the girl said.

'And that means we gotta screw?'

'I think that's the best way to get pregnant,' the girl smiled. 'Then, if we are successful, we will beg you to impregnate the other girls who are now in suspension.'

Blackie licked his lips. 'How many are there?'

'About three hundred.'

That was enough for him, that bastard, Knight, and the Captain, too, if the Captain would lower himself to helping a bunch of helpless girls.

'You'll be known as the savior of our race, Blackie,' the girl said, coming toward him, swaying her hips under the little skirt which just covered her business. 'And I'll make it very interesting for you.'

'I'll bet you will,' Blackie said, getting a hard on just from looking at her tits. They were longish tits of a fullness which stretched the brown aureola at the tip of each hanging beauty. The nipples were almost flush with the swollen milk wagons and the silver paint made a bright, erotic contrast with her soft-looking white skin. She had long eyelashes and dark eyes of a brownness almost black. Her nose was long and regal and her mouth was full. Her lower lip protruded a tiny bit, just enough to chew on. She was long in the waist and her waist was very thin. Her legs, extending from under the skimpy skirt, were long and perfect.

'I'll bet you'll make it interesting,' Blackie said. 'Well, baby, I guess the best thing we can do is go inside and get at it. If I'm gonna be known as the savior of your race, I'd better get started.' He took her arm and guided her into the ship, past the control room, down the corridor. 'Three hundred of you, huh? All as pretty as you?'

'I am considered ordinary by most of the members of my race, who are truly beautiful.'

'I don't believe it,' Blackie said. 'Three hundred huh? Prettier than you?' *My aching ass*, he thought. Then he thought about why not let the *Swinger* swing on home, leaving him, the father of his race, old Adam all over again, with his three hundred lovelies. It would be the work of a lifetime and then there'd be the daughters, his daughters. And, since he was establishing a race, it wouldn't be incest. Not really.

'Hey, baby,' he said. 'There are two other guys, er, males, on board this bucket. But they're both ball-less, see? I mean they can't get no kids because they've been cut. I mean they're sterile. You dig?'

'I dig, Blackie,' she said, stepping into his quarters ahead of him. 'Then it's only you, isn't it? You'll have to do it all, Blackie.'

'Gee, well, I dunno. I mean, it'll be a strain. Three hundred! Boy, it'll be a – wham – boom – ahhhh – I mean, it'll be a hard night's work, baby, but I'll do my best.' He laughed. 'I might just die trying.'

The girl looked at him with a quickness which was lost on Blackie because he was coming out of his one-piece. She smiled, shrugged and wiggled her hips and stood nude before him. The box, like her head, was covered by blonde locks and he looked at it to see if it was put on sideways or something. After all, the broad was an alien.

114

But it was just a common, ordinary looking box and when she bumped it at him he let his clothes fall to the floor and started toward her. She fell languidly onto the bunk, rolled, her back flat, her lower body twisted. This position showed the rise of her hips, the crack of her fine looking ass and the hugeness of one breast, for it barely sank, even though she was lying flat. Most broads lying on their backs, lost most of their headlights. They just fell down under their arms or flattened out or something. Not this one.

Then she, after giving him the view of her ass, rolled back and spread her legs as if she were very, very eager. She pulled up her knees slightly and spread her thighs and the twitch looked out at him wetly and dankly with one little eye. He lunged at her, so hot was he.

'That's it, lover,' she said, 'be rough. Give it to me. Throw it to me, Blackie. Ah!' For she was stabbed in the groin as Blackie missed and she wiggled and moved and thrust her hand down between their bodies to insert him in pre-lubed hotness which swallowed him. Then she was a tiger, throwing her legs up around his back and hunching like a maniac as he threw it to her.

'Stop, darling!' she cried. 'Wait!' He paused in mid-stroke, then eased up into her to feel his probe touching hard internal organs. 'Ah,' she moaned. 'Ah, yes!'

'You goin' already?'

'No, darling! Oh, no! I'm feeling your sperm!'

'But I ain't come yet,' Blackie said.

'I feel them. They're oozing out slightly, only a few, but I feel them and – '

'What do you mean, you feel them?'

'Oh, poor darling. I forgot. You don't know. We, my race, have this thing. We have control over all our cells so that we can control them and I'm using this sensitivity to feel the sperm coming out of you and they're friendly sperm, compatible sperm. I can feel them seeking my egg – '

'Jesus!' Blackie said, pumping her like crazy. 'You can feel all that? You can control your body down to cellular level?'

'Yes, darling. And it's a gift which can be learned. I can help.'

'Later,' Blackie said, plunging his dagger deep into her vitals. 'I'm busy right now making you some more sperm to hunt your little egg.'

And the strangest thing was happening. Each stroke Blackie took seemed to drive him deeper and deeper. He could feel the base of his probe being engulfed in the hot, soft, exciting folds of her cunt. He'd never been so deep in a woman in his life. 'Ahhhhhhggggg,' he moaned, but held back. 'What you do to me, baby!'

'You like?' She pulled down on him with her legs and then pulled them all the way up to put them over his shoulders. He felt his balls being kissed by the wetness of her.

'Gaaa,' he said. And the hard, wet, pulsings began in her vagina, squeezing him. He felt her enclosing him, taking his testes into her. He felt her surround all his manhood with woman-pussy and he thought he'd die with the goodness. 'What? What?' he gasped.

'I can control myself, darling. See?' And a soft-hard lubricated something slipped into his rear, went up gently, massaged his glands up there and, as he bucked and pumped, all enclosed in that warm, squeezing pussy, he was being buggered by that soft, gentle thing and he knew when he popped he was going to blow a hole in her womb. There was so much pussy. His whole lower body seemed to be pushing into pussy and it was grand and glorious.

'Good, baby?' she asked.

116

'The only way it could be better is if I had a dork two feet long,' he gasped.

He felt himself growing. He didn't know how it happened and he didn't take time to care because he felt himself growing, pushing, pushing, until he was up her to her navel and then further and further until it was incredible.

'It ain't real,' he said, gasping. When he pulled back it seemed as if he went on for miles and then when he gave it to her it went and went and went.

'It's real,' she said. 'I've been helping you. Here, with me, you can control yourself as I can control my body. You can make it bigger – *bigger* – '

'But – you – hurt – '

'No, darling. I can become a giant vagina. I can take it. Make it bigger – bigger – bigger!'

He let it grow in width until it stretched her fearfully, until it was huge and long and then he was pumping and he felt himself being swallowed by her. He felt himself becoming one huge penis and there was a time when he was in her up to his chin, pumping, pumping. He put his hand up and she was huge, her clitoris as big as a basketball and he fondled it with both hands and she came, long, squeezing joy in her. All she was was a giant vagina and he was in her up to his armpits playing with her huge clitoris as she squeezed his penis-body and then he let himself grow until they were, together, larger than the *Swinger*. He was a huge weapon and he was fucking the whole world and the whole world was a sweet, pulsing, continuously climaxing vagina and when he went his whole body strained and pumped and she screamed with joy and told him, breathlessly, as they came back to their normal shape, that his sperm was in the womb and that one was nearing the egg and then there was a breathless moment of suspense and she screamed and fainted. She

117

awoke and said, 'I'm impregnated. Our genes are compatible. You will be begged to do this with all three hundred of us.'

That excited Blackie so much that he told her he wanted her to be a cooch as big as the Grand Canyon and he would be all dick and eight miles long and they were off and running. When she bit him in her joy he laughed, for he was having sex as no man, he thought, before him had ever had sex. Then she had to leave and he went outside, weak, sapped, and fell asleep.

14

Lt Ellie Martin, medofficer of the *Swinger*, made her way to what had once been a hospital, judging from the equipment she had seen during her first scouting trip into the city. Inside the huge building, which had been built with marble floors and walls of some permanent, plastic-like material, the little rooms were arranged much as they were in an Earth hospital. Ellie made a few unrewarding side trips into individual rooms before she discovered the surgery. There she found a wealth of material to interest her. Stainless metal tools were in their containers, looking new as the day they were last sterilized.

She spent an hour in the surgery, taking notes, collecting objects to be taken back to the ship, making an Instaflex record of all interesting equipment. Then she went exploring and found the room where there was life.

She heard, first, the distant purr of machinery. Her heart stopped. She paused in her purposeful stroll down a long corridor and listened. There was definite sound on a world where the only sounds, to now, had been made by the wind, the water or the crew of the earthship. She considered calling the others, but decided that she, after all, was a commissioned officer in the space service and was capable of handling an investigation of the sound of distant machines. She deposited all of her equipment and the objects she'd taken from the surgery on the dusty floor of the deserted corridor and proceeded cautiously toward the distant hum. She could tell she was getting closer and, when she stood before a door, painted red, she knew the sounds came from within.

With her heart beating fast and holding her breath, she tried the door. It opened and she looked into a room filled with impressive machinery. There were a dozen long, high box-like objects placed uniformly around the room and the humming sounds came from them. She entered, her hand on the butt of the blaster strapped to her hips, and looked down through a clear cover into the face of the most handsome man she'd ever seen. He was lying on his back on the long, high platform which was roughly the size of a single bed. His eyes were closed. He did not breathe. Quickly, she explored the rest of the room and equally handsome, still men were under the covers of the other eleven contraptions.

Heart pounding with excitement, she looked for some clue. Surely, she thought, they were in suspension. Else, why enclose them in the clear covers? Why the humming machines? Surely they were alive, suspended, saved by the dying civilization of this world to be revived by someone, someday. But how?

The answer to her question was so obvious she had missed it. On the rear wall, done in a simple, universal sign and picture language, were instructions.

Ellie debated the advisability of undertaking the thawing-out process alone, without having someone standing by to help her if the revived men were – She smiled. No. She could tell by looking at the handsome men under glass that they were a gentle race, a civilized race. They had waited for centuries for someone to come to revive them and she wouldn't make them wait another hour. She picked a case at random. It happened to be the first one inside the door, the first she'd seen, the one which contained a man so handsome she couldn't believe it. He was perfect in every detail. He had a body which would make the healthiest earthman jealous and a beautiful face and, she noted it dispassionately, a large priapus which lay at ease, hanging over one thigh. He would be the first.

She followed the picture instructions, pushing buttons in careful sequence. The machinery within the case increased its tempo and a cloud of something obscured her view for a moment. She felt heat emanating from the case, which had been cold to the touch before. More buttons. The cover of the case slid back and he was lying there still. She touched him tentatively. His flesh was cold and he was not breathing. She wondered if she had failed. But as she watched, his chest rose, heaved, gasped, and a regular pattern of breathing began. She looked to the picture wall for more instruction. There was only one left. The last instruction, unexplained, told her to raise the body temperature of the man by three units. But how? She looked. No more buttons. The temperature of the room was controlled by some hidden machines of which she knew nothing.

Panicky, she searched for some means and hit upon an age-old device. Trembling, she crawled up on the platform. It was comfortably padded. She lowered herself atop the quiet man and put her weight on him, holding him tightly in her arms. Since the beginning of time woman had warmed man thusly. If that was what it took to revive the handsome alien, that she would do.

She watched his face. Nothing. He breathed but did not move otherwise. She felt his hard-muscled body, his chest, his flat stomach, the soft mass of his penis under her. She was desperately afraid she was not warming him. In haste, she opened her one-piece to put the softness of her body, her own personal heat in contact with his nudeness. He felt cool, but not cold. She squirmed, trying to will him into life.

And the first evidence of life made her giggle. Nothing moved but the large weapon, which was lying in contact with her stomach. It throbbed. It hardened. It pushed into her soft stomach and she giggled again, because she didn't know the man, knew him only as an alien being, and here she was lying atop him, her arms around him, and him becoming hard in response to her body heat.

But if that was what it took!

She held him, felt the big, exciting hardness reach full growth, pushed against her bare stomach. Surely, now, he could open his eyes. But he didn't. She moved against him, trying to put more of her life-giving warmth against him. He was so big down there he was about to push through her stomach, so she wiggled down, let the big weapon go up between her legs and that was a mistake, for she was a woman, a passionate woman, and in the excitement of exploring the planet, she'd been neglecting her homework with Blackie and John Knight. She felt that huge thing between her thighs, lying lengthwise along her slit and said slit began to come to life, lubricating itself.

She giggled. She had remembered the medical fact that intercourse with a woman is one of the finest ways to raise a subnormal body temperature in a man. She giggled, also, because she was seriously considering inserting that monstrous weapon in her lubricous cockpit.

Well, she thought, why not?

It would be like the old fairy story of Prince Charming, bringing Snow White or whoever the hell it was back to life with a kiss.

She raised herself, reached down and grasped that huge giggle stick with a shaking hand and stabbed it into her tool box with a downward movement of her body. It filled her to splitting. It went and went and she gasped with delight as she felt things touched inside. She'd never, never been so well filled. Blackie Decker had a big one, but this was unbelievable. She hurt and spasmed with joy

122

at the same time and, for a long time, she just lay there, impaled to the core, and soaked in it. It was a bit necrophilic, she decided, but her body had taken over and she was hotter than a virgin at an orgy. All alone with the sleeping man, filled with his hugeness, she moved. Then she did a daring thing. She sat up on him. She was kneeling a-straddle of him and it almost tore her apart it was so deep in her; and then she began to raise and lower herself. She bounced up and down, taking that huge wonder in deeper each time, all the time gasping and crying with a mixture of pain and joy and – oh! – he moved! He opened his eyes and smiled. She stopped, on the verge of paroxysmal climax. Then he reached up, took her in his arms, pulled her down on him and killed her embarrassment with a tongue kiss which sent shivers of delight through her. His big, gentle hands went down, cupped around the rounded points of her rump, held her close; and his body lunged up and up, filling her and bringing her to the point of climax and she burst open like a ripe melon and melted down around the hugeness of his prick and throbbed and spasmed with a big, big, big, vaginal climax and he didn't even slow down, taking her with him up another hill of joy.

'Good?' he asked, along the way.

'Oh, good,' she moaned. 'So big!'

'Like it bigger?'

'Oh, no! I couldn't stand it!'

'Yes,' he said. 'Yes.' And he grew. She took it as it swelled in her, until it was the size of her forearm, stretching, stretching, pushing up into her vitals and sending multiple climaxes through her shaking body. She knew it was medically impossible. She knew she couldn't stand an organ of that size without suffering damage but she took it and wanted more, gasping, fighting for more.

'It's mental,' she said. 'Hallucinatory.'

'Real,' he said. 'It's all real. I've opened up an unused portion of your brain and you can alter the shape, the makeup of your body. You're doing it now.'

The medical and intellectual excitement of such a fantastic thing was secondary to her sexual excitement. She let him grow until she was only a hollow shell of a woman, a woman filled with penis to her throat and then, with inspiration, she altered that, too, and took the head of it into her mouth from the inside and caressed it with her tongue as spasm after spasm of orgasm left her weak and quaking.

'Will you help me wake the others now?' he asked, as they lay in each other's arms, back to normal.

'I couldn't. I just couldn't. I'm so tired. So very, very wonderfully tired.'

He merely smiled. 'Yes, you can. I'll help you.'

In two minutes she felt the renewed assault of lust. She helped him revive another man, holding him in her arms until the organ between his legs gave the first sign of waking. Then, the first one in her eager mouth, the second one in her newly activated living cush, she made the man live. After that there were more men and, at one time, she herself made multiple quims and took several men at once in hairy, lubricous openings in her thighs, her shoulders, her back.

Finally, no mind acrobatics could conquer the bone weariness, and she told them she must go back to the ship to report that she'd found life on the planet.

15

Lt John Knight met the Gant in an art gallery in the form of a statue of a man screwing himself. Knight had been walking for a couple of hours, seeing a lot of beautiful things, collecting a few, when he came upon the statue in a room all by itself. The man depicted was handsome in body, strange in dick, for it was long enough so that the man in the statue could suck himself without bending his back or his neck. To Knight, who had often wondered what it would be like to be able to give one's self a blow job, it was an erotic thing.

He looked at the statue for a long time, feeling an erection. Then, upon close inspection, he discovered that the mouth of the statue was not a man's mouth at all. It was a vagina with *labia* and a clitoris and what he'd thought was a moustache was pubic hair growing under the nose of the man-thing. He gasped. That was an even more erotic notion. A man who was both male and female.

Hell, he didn't have any hidden homosexual tendencies. Men weren't his bag, but the idea of having a cooch of one's own and a big whang to stick it in, also one's own, was the sexiest thing he'd ever seen.

Then he saw the pictures on the wall, studied them for a moment, followed them to a small recess in the wall and realized with pounding heart that the pictures were instructions and, if he were right, if he were reading them right, there was something in the recess in the wall to allow *him* or anyone else to do what the statue was doing.

He looked. There was a small metal box. He opened it.

Inside there was a pill. He told himself he was crazy, that he was taking a desperate chance. The pill had been there for centuries and would have lost its strength.

But there was something which told him, forced him, urged him until he swallowed the pill with a gulp, felt no change immediately and then felt a tickle on his upper lip and put his hand there to find hair. He didn't feel any different, but his lips ran vertically now and instead of a tongue he felt, with his finger, an iris-like opening; above the opening he found the clit and, at last, knew how it felt to be a woman and the thrill was so immense that he had to sit down.

There was a couch. He hadn't noticed it before, but now it was handy and he sank down on it, fingering his clit and feeling the thrills he'd never imagined and he remembered he was a man and shot one hand down into his one-piece and felt it huge and hot, dripping eagerness. He saw the queer statue and wished devoutly that his ordinary sized weapon would grow and it did. He saw it come up toward him, snake-like, little eye oozing excitement. He felt the answering thrill in his mouth-vagina and then it was touching and he doubled himself, felt his long, huge wick enter his pulsing, hungry snatch and kept it going until he was like a Mobius strip all inside and no outside, fucking himself deep so that the tip almost met the base inside him and it was the most heavenly thing; he just lay on the couch and rolled into a ball of quivering, leaping, thrusting passion and filled himself with spoutings.

The Gant, who delighted in excess, found John Knight to be his favorite of all the creatures from the ship. He concentrated, did Knight, and the Gant liked that. The Gant lived it, one huge, unending, lustful, greedy climax to orgasm and felt the joy only a Gant can know.

In its pleasure with John Knight, the Gant almost

126

goofed. For he left Lt Boots Pastele alone in a library with locked film cabinets which had been hermetically sealed. Boots solved the lock easily, found the film clips inside to be preserved perfectly by the scientific enclosure, found, also, that the enclosed projector was working and started the film running. There was a narrative, but she couldn't understand it. The language sounded like a mixture of German, birdcalls and grunts but she was sure that, given time, she'd find the key to it. There were other sealed containers which would bear investigation, containing perhaps, microfilm of the printed word of this world.

The film, however, caught her attention. It showed a huge ship moving away into space. It was an important trip or a first trip or something, for the crowd was large and important looking people, very humanoid, were there making speeches and waving. Then the ship was coming back and the crowd was there and there was music and noise and great joy.

The ports opened after the ship had settled into its gantry and there was a hush. Then, after a long, long pause, men moved forward, disappeared into the ship and came out bearing a lifeless body.

The camera shifted, suddenly, to show a group of people near the ship engaging in wild, orgiastic sex. Bare bodies gleamed in the sun. Women writhed as they were penetrated and, as the camera stayed on the group, more and more people fell into the tangle of limbs and bodies until hundreds were performing all the sexual acts imaginable.

Boots was both shocked and puzzled. Was it some religious ritual! Was the wild sex of the crowd connected in some way with the lifeless body which the men had carried out of the ship?

She reversed the film, watched the beginning again. Then she let it run through and, after the mass orgy at the

127

ship, saw other orgies and single couples and trios and groups, all engaging in sex. They screwed in cars, on the streets, in offices, in parks. The voice of the narrator sounded sad, somehow.

Boots suddenly remembered the two small rodents who had screwed themselves to death. She watched the efforts of a couple on the screen in close-up and saw their struggles grow weak. The man continued to move for a while after it was evident that the woman, his partner in excess, was unconscious and the whole thing seemed, suddenly, sinister and threatening.

Then the Gant moved its attention from the wildly self-fornicating John Knight, the enlarged penis that was Blackie Decker, the sincere Captain, who was screwing his eleven-year-old wife, and the passion-drunk Ellie Martin.

The film was no longer sinister to Boots. It was the wildest pornographic film ever made. They still had a few of them on Earth and they had never excited Boots before, but this film of mass screwing, close-up screwing, sucking and muff diving and all conceivable sexual combinations set fire surging into her pants and she began to masturbate breathlessly as she watched a world screw. She urged herself on to climax after climax and when she left the library, spent, tired, feeling slightly ashamed, she wobbled as she walked. It had been the most sexually satisfying afternoon of her life, masturbating all alone there as she watched the film. Why, then, did she feel uneasy?

16

Finding Sergeant Decker asleep while on guard took Capt. Asa Smith's mind off the pleasant debauch with his astrally projected wife. He woke the sergeant, chewed him out considerably and decided then and there that it was time to get some discipline back into his crew.

'Captain,' Blackie said, having endured the lecture, 'are you finished?'

'Why you – ' He couldn't speak further.

''Cause if you are, baby, I got news for you. We're not alone on this planet. There's three hundred gorgeous babies – '

'Have you been drinking, in addition to sleeping on duty?'

'Come off it, Sir, this is important. There's three hundred of 'em and they've been in suspension and they want me – us – to replenish the race by impregnating them and I got one this afternoon and impregnated her and – '

'You what?' Smith asked, 'you what?'

'Impregnated her. Knocked her up. You know.'

'Perhaps, Sergeant,' said the Captain, feeling a strange tightening at the back of his neck, 'we'd better go inside and have a full report on this.'

Inside, Blackie repeated the whole story, leaving out no erotic detail. When he came to the part about being able to make himself a penis as big as the world the Captain squinted and remembered the strangeness of Elenore's ability to be any age. He looked down at his finger and there was Elenore's ring, the one he'd given

129

her. There could be no mistaking it. And yet, while he was enjoying his wife all the way from her present age back to the age of eleven, Sgt Decker had been experiencing an equally strange thing, being able to make his penis grow to fantastic size.

Then Lt Martin came in, excited about having revived the last twelve men in the entire planet and Lt Knight came in, strangely exhausted and uncommunicative and Lt Pastele had a strange tale about a wildly sexy film showing a whole world fucking.

The Captain closed all doors and checked all systems and ran a check for alien presence on the *Swinger*. His check showed nothing, for the Gant – not a physical being in the sense we recognize it – was undetectable. But the Gant was there. It was there in John Knight's quarters having dessert as Knight grew his mouth-pussy and fucked himself into exhausted sleep and it was there in the quarters of the others as the Captain stood watch and thought. With Decker, Pastele and Martin, the Gant took its measure of orgasm in an inspired threesome in the sergeant's quarters. Pastele and Martin were drawn there by huge physical urges, against all common sense. Martin took Decker's probe and found that it seemed to be bigger. In fact, Decker found that he could make it bigger, but not nearly as big as it had been during the afternoon with the blonde native of the planet. Pastele, fighting against the overwhelming urge, kissed both Decker and Martin while they screwed, tickled the sergeant's balls with her fingers and sat on Decker's face to have a satisfactory climax on his mouth.

Only Capt. Asa Smith resisted the insidious onslaught of the most sensuous creature in the universe, the Gant. He was on duty. He would not let himself think of Elenore. He was so firm that the Gant gave up on him temporarily. The Gant did not want to rouse suspicions, not until it had gained transportation back to the planet from which these creatures came. Their minds transmitted the fact that the Earth had billions of entities. And the image of a billion orgasms at once made the Gant cringe with joy.

During the night, when Lt Martin failed to relieve the Captain at the appointed time, he left control to look for her. Pastele, exhausted, had retired, leaving Martin and Decker screwing in Decker's room. So exhausted was Pastele that she left the ship's door ajar and the Captain, not having located Martin in her room and suspecting the worst, looked in to see the two, officer and enlisted man, screwing energetically.

Asa Smith was angry as he called his entire crew to control. He used shipscan, with proper warning. He saw Knight lying exhausted on his bed, nude, his lax weapon in his hand. He saw Pastele sprawled on her cot, nude and exhausted. He had already confronted the sergeant and the medofficer and they stood before him sheepishly. He read the regulations to them. He advised them that they were all under technical arrest and were confined to the ship and to their quarters while not on duty. He forbade further sexual activity on the pain of instant death via the Captain's blaster. Knight smiled weakly. With his new gift he had no need for sexual activity with female officers. That bastard, Decker, was the one who would suffer on the way home. Martin felt guilty and Decker cursed under his breath and vowed to jump ship so he could establish a race by impregnating three hundred beautiful virgins. Pastele felt sick, saddened by the situation, aware of her excesses. Something nagged at her consciousness and she couldn't quite bring it into focus.

The Gant, angered by the Captain's interruption of its joys through the screwing of the sergeant and Lt Martin, put such a huge load of charge into the Captain's penis

131

that he thought erotically of his wife and shot off right there before the crew. Fortunately, however, Asa Smith wore thick service underwear which soaked up the discharge.

But the Gant was not to be denied. Capt. Asa Smith, prude, hardhead, strong-minded man who was true to his wife (who, incidentally, having never been within light-years of Smith's Planet, had ventured into Lesbianism and was, at that moment, being serviced by a butch with a huge dildo) would not spoil the Gant's pleasure. True, the safest course for the Gant was to lie low. Board the ship – and it was already partially aboard – ride the space miles home to the planet of a billion simultaneous orgasms. But caution was not the nature of the Gant. It wanted a billion orgasms, but it wanted a few little orgasms immediately, it wanted to enjoy Knight fucking himself and it wanted to service the female of solid, male projections of portions of itself and it wanted to break into the will of the Captain.

So, for a long night, the Gant did battle with Capt. Asa Smith. And, although the Gant could activate the ejaculation process in Smith, it could not break through the iron reserve, for Smith had deduced that there was something, something weird on his planet and he was not going to indulge in any more of what he had come to believe was hallucinatory sex.

So, the Gant decided to sacrifice the Captain. Since he was physical, and not, therefore, within range of the Gant's personal powers of destruction, powers which eons past had depopulated the universe of other Gants so that all orgasms could belong to *The* Gant, the Gant planted into the Captain's mind an undeniable urge to make one more scouting trip into the dead city outside.

'You ain't goin' out there in the dark, are you, Captain?' Blackie Decker asked.

'I have to, Sergeant,' Asa Smith said, not really knowing why. 'I'm leaving you in charge. And, Sergeant, there's something out there, you know. I want you to stand guard. Let nothing pass. If it isn't me, I don't care if it's your beautiful blonde or Lt Martin's beautiful men, you blast them, do you understand? There's something sinister going on here.'

Asa Smith went out into the dark before dawn and Blackie stood guard. He had all the sensory systems operational and, therefore, picked up the approach of the girls via instrument before he saw them. He used the outside amplification system and ordered them to stay.

'Blackie, darling,' said the one he'd impregnated. 'It is I. I have brought others for you. Others for you to impregnate.'

Blackie used the scanner and saw them, a line of lush lovelies in itty bitty skirts with bare breasts, all lovely, all such ravishing beauties that he had a nut ache just thinking about knocking all of them up.

'Look, girls.' He didn't even know her name. 'I'm in hot water with the old man. I'm confined to the ship.'

'We can come in.'

'Naw, I got orders.'

'Then *you* come out, Blackie. Stay here with us. Be the father of a new race.' She pushed forward a delectable little redhead. 'She has drawn the lot to be the first, Blackie. Look at her. See how young she is, how pretty. And virgin, Blackie, but passionate. Very passionate.'

'Yeah, I'm looking,' Blackie said, getting hard at the thoughts of knocking up that one.

'You can stay with us,' she went on. 'Let the ship go to Earth without you. Stay with us and be honored. Be the father of your country. Stay with us and love us, Blackie.'

'Stay with us, Blackie,' the others begged.

Only a lifetime of devotion to the service kept him from

bolting then, kept him from running out the hatch, joining them. 'Look, girls,' he said. 'I will. I'll stay. I promise you that. But first I gotta talk to the Captain, tell him how it is. He'll understand.'

'He won't let you stay, Blackie. He'll make you go back.'

'No, he's a reasonable man. He'll understand why I'm needed here.'

'He will make you go back to Earth with him,' she said, her voice sad. 'And I have waked all of them. All three hundred of my sisters, and only I am impregnated. The race will surely die. All our hopes, all the work of the ancients will be wasted.'

'No,' Blackie said. 'I promise. The race won't die. I'll stay.' He was out of the ship before he realized it. Around him, the pale light of dawn showed him the girls, dozens of them, hundreds of them, all bare-breasted, all beautiful. 'You see,' he said. 'I'm coming with you now.'

'Hush,' one of them said. 'He is coming.'

'We will await you,' the prime girl told him. 'Come to us, if you can, and you must, in the large park in the city.'

Then they were gone.

'Why are you out of the ship, Decker?' Capt. Asa Smith asked harshly.

'Captain, I well, you see, I, they – '

'Get inside, Decker. Now.'

'No, Captain, I ain't going. I'm staying. I'm staying here on this planet.'

'You've gone crazy, Sergeant. Whatever this thing is that is on this planet, it's got to you. You're going, all right, if I have to – ' He reached for his blaster.

'Don't do it, Captain,' Blackie begged, his own hand on the butt of his blaster. 'Don't try to outdraw me. I'm the fastest blaster in the universe.'

134

'Are you saying you would resist if I ordered you to re-enter the ship?'

'That's what I'm saying, Cap'n. Don't force it, huh? There's a lot more at stake here than you realize.'

'Sergeant,' Capt. Asa Smith said, slowly putting his hand on his blaster and beginning to draw it from the holster. 'I'm ordering you to board the ship. If you refuse, I'll be forced to blast you down.'

'Don't Cap'n Smith, please don't,' Blackie pleaded, watching fearfully as the weapon came slowly out of the Captain's holster. 'I can't let you do this. There's a whole race at stake.'

Blackie, *Blackie, Blackie*. He could hear them calling. They were waiting.

He blasted Asa Smith before the Captain could squeeze the trigger. He waited until the last possible second and then he drew with blinding speed and killed Smith because he read in Smith's eyes that the Captain was going to live up to his word. The Captain was going to force him back aboard the *Swinger* or kill him; and he had a race to father.

'Oh, no,' Lt Boots Pastele moaned, coming out to see the stump which had been the Captain fall with a grisly thud to the downtrodden grass. 'Oh, God, no!'

'I didn't want to do it, Lieutenant. He made me. He was gonna make me go back.'

'Go back? Do you mean you want to stay here?'

She tried to keep her eyes off the charred mass which had been Asa Smith, trying also to watch Blackie, who was backing away.

'Take the ship home, Lieutenant,' Blackie said, 'and when you get back, tell them back there that there's a whole new race of people out here, waiting for contact with the Earth. And tell 'em that they'll have to do

135

business with Blackie Decker. You tell 'em that, you hear?'

When he was gone, Boots went sadly into the ship. She found Ellie and John Knight sixty-nining each other, a little sidelight of amusement for the Gant while it observed the incident outside the ship and while it followed Blackie to the park where three hundred nubile girls waited to be knocked up. In gratitude to the sergeant, the Gant would play with him as long as the mental force could be projected back to what the creatures called Smith's Planet. For a few weeks, until the earthbound ship was too far distant, Blackie Decker would enjoy a happy existence. Then, just before the ship passed out of range, the Gant would have the sergeant enjoy one long, endless orgasm ending in –

'Goddamnit,' Boots shouted, 'knock it off. The Captain's been killed and Decker has gone ape and deserted.'

'Ummmofff,' Ellie said, her mouth filled with an expanded Knight tool. 'Gaaaaa,' she repeated.

'Ummknicck,' Knight said weakly, his face buried in Ellie's crotch.

There was that sinister, threatening feeling. With quick determination, Lt Boots Pastele ran a check, found all systems 'go', and headed the *Swinger* for home, back toward Alpha Bötes, accelerating outward from Smith's Planet, through the crowded starlanes of the Orion Arm. She knew that something was terribly, terribly wrong. She wanted to go home.

So did the Gant.

17

Because there was so much at stake, the Gant kept sex to a near-normal level. He indulged in living normal screwings between Lt Martin and Lt Knight. He took the risk now and then of having a sweet, wonderful lay with Lt Pastele and Lt Knight, but he didn't push Pastele. It knew of the knowledge buried just below the conscious level in her mind. It knew of her doubts and her latent morality. Ahead of it were billions of entities, all eager to copulate, all waiting for the ultimate sexual stimulus, the Gant. And it knew that Lt Boots Pastele, with the knowledge in her head and with her computers, was its only chance of ever getting to that paradise, Earth.

However, the days were long for the impatient Gant, so it amused itself by living the double orgasms of Lt Knight as he fucked himself. Then, five months and twenty days out from Smith's Planet, ten days before J-day, the Gant got excited and greedy and had John Knight suffer one gigantic orgasm too many and Lt John Knight died, a happy, ejaculating man.

They put the body in suspension, the two lieutenants saddened and lonely. For five days the Gant lay low until its urges were uncontrollable. Then it instigated a woman-woman scene between Ellie and Boots, had a few orgasms and stopped just in time, since Ellie's heart was not holding up too well under the strain of pure pleasure in the form of Gant-controlled Gant-amplified orgasms in multiple units. Weak, tired to near the point of death, Ellie took to her bed with massive doses of vitamins and antibiotics, which did little good.

Alone with Lt Pastele, the Gant had her masturbate a few times, being very careful. He could sense her questions.

The Gant made its final mistake only two days before the big J. Ellie, recovered enough to sit weakly in the control room with Boots, used Gant power to turn her left leg into a giant, prehensile penis and began to screw herself.

'Oh, God,' Boots said. 'Oh, God.'

The Gant, in the form of a golden man-god, stood before her, unable to withhold itself from her for another minute.

'You're – you're what's happening,' Boots said, reaching for her blaster.

'I am happening,' the Gant said. 'Feel!'

And for a moment she felt the thrill of the huge penis in Ellie's crack. For a moment she shared the lustful fun, the unbelievable joy of having her body filled with penis made up from one's self. Then, with his power, the Gant made her feel the last days of Smith's Planet – the vast, worldwide, simultaneous orgasm which had sated the Gant for decades. It was the most tremendous release of sexual energy known since the Gant lived a primitive planet of a few billion souls into a terminal orgasm far out on the rim of the galaxy. It was so huge, so tremendous –

'You did it,' she breathed, weak, flushed, her body feeling like molten joy. 'You did it until they were all – '

'A regrettable mistake,' the Gant said. 'An error I won't make again.'

'You want to do that to Earth,' Boots said.

'No, darling. No. Never again. Good though it was.' And again she felt the huge, multi-million person orgasm and it left her panting. 'For that was followed by this!' And she felt the Gant's centuries of frustration. The pain of it, the sheer sexual need of it, dizzied her.

138

'I don't want that again,' the Gant said, through his golden man-god. 'Do you think I want *that*? No, I will not live the Earth. I will be moderate. I will enjoy the natural orgasms. I will not be greedy.'

'You're doing that – that – obscene thing to Ellie,' she said, feeling that terrible urge, that centuries old frustration.

'Would you like me to stop it?'

'Yes, please.'

Ellie stopped. Her leg became a leg and she fainted.

'What are you?' Boots asked, looking at the golden man-god.

'I am the Gant. I am one form of life – a concentrated, specialized, immortal form of life. I am the beginning and the end, alpha and omega. I am – '

She got the flash of thought before he cut it off. ' – one continuous orgasm, concentrated into unbelievable intensity, but released only in the presence of true orgasm on a physical plane.'

'I won't take you to Earth,' she said. 'I won't turn you loose on the Earth to do what you did on Smith's Planet.'

'I anticipated that,' he said. Again she felt the giant, mass orgasm and the thrill was more than she could have taken had she not been reinforced by the Gant. 'I offer you that. I give you continuous pleasure, immortal joy. I will make you my bride. We will share and share alike and my joys will be your joys.'

He caught her in his arms, that golden man-god which was only one minor form of the Gant. He made love to her. It wasn't screwing, as pleasure seekers screw or fucking as animals fuck. It was making Love. It was tender and sweet and very damned complete and she had a monstrously wonderful orgasm.

'That I offer,' he said, 'continuously, eternally. You have only to take me to Earth.'

139

Ellie stirred and moaned. 'Oh, Ellie,' Boots cried, confused. 'Help me. Help me.'

'She can't help you,' the Gant told her. 'Look.'

And before her yes-saying eyes, as she shared the Gant's delight, she watched Ellie fuck herself to death with a huge, self-formed penis and a glorious climax that lasted hours before the weak heart finally quit.

'You've killed her,' she said, weakly, sadly.

'She could never help you. She was one of the ordinary ones. Now it is only you and I, partners, mates, enjoying the orgasms of a race together.'

It was J-Day. The Gant had loved her tenderly, gently, satisfyingly, for hours. She felt glorious. She could look down through the years to endless pleasure. She made her calculations and prepared for the big jump which would put them within six months travel of the Earth, six months which would be an endless delight with the golden Gant to show her more and more pleasure. The Gant could show her nerves in her body, could create sensations which she'd never even dreamed of and the Gant, with his memory, could show her mass orgasm and tremendous, debauched, terrible, gusty, unending climax.

'You must leave me alone,' she said, pushing the golden, man-god away from between her legs, where he was moving his tongue swish-swish swiftly over her aching clit. 'I have to have a clear head if I'm going to jump.'

So he left her alone and she checked and re-checked and she was sure the computers were right and were ready to make the jump and her mind was clear of carnal pleasures for the first time in months.

T'was then that she remembered the film she'd seen in a dead library on a dead planet, thousands, millions of fornicating people, fucking themselves into oblivion. Was that to happen to Earth? The Gant promised that he would not, as he called it, live the Earth and to the Gant 'living' was having the continual orgasm of all beings until their frail bodies failed under the strain of pure pleasure. Could she believe the Gant? He or it was uncontrolled and greedy. He or it had an infinite capacity for orgasm and once on Earth he, or it, might go berserk as it had on Smith's Planet and then she'd be a co-destroyer of her world, experiencing every single orgasm as the human race and all living things which copulated fucked themselves to death.

On the other hand, she had the power to keep the Gant away from the Earth. There were two sets of jump controls on the *Swinger*. One was an emergency spare. It could be switched in instantly. With either set of jump controls she could send the ship off into uncharted space and not even the Gant could travel across the light-years of space. She could keep the Gant from Earth by losing herself and the Gant in space together and –

She wondered what he would do if she tricked him. She had seen the way Ellie died. She had glimpsed, through the mind of the Gant, the desolate Sgt Blackie Decker, dying in continuous paroxysms of climax, back on Smith's Planet. She could imagine what would happen to her if she marooned the Gant in space. He'd live her and live her and keep her alive until –

She set a completely random setting on the spare jump control. As J-Hour approached, she watched the chronometer nervously and tried to make up her mind. She wasn't a particularly brave girl. She didn't want to die, fucked to death by the Gant in some insane way, like Ellie. Nor did she want to unleash the Gant on Earth. She was a sensuous girl who enjoyed ordinary climax, but not necessarily the unbelievable climaxes which could be shared with the Gant if she took him to Earth.

At J-minus five minutes, she was still undecided.

The Golden Gant, in man-form, kissed her ear tenderly. 'Stop it,' she whispered. 'I must concentrate.'

The Gant had promised poor Blackie a chance to be the father of a race.

The Gant was the most romantic, most wonderful, most sensual being of all time and she could share its infinite capacity for pleasure. She could live the Earth with the Gant or she could face an angry, vengeful Gant in the small, lonely ship lost in deep space.

'Oh, God,' she prayed to the neoreligious deity of her parents, the God man had killed back in the twentieth century and had not been too successful in reviving. 'Oh, God.'

And at J-minus thirty seconds and counting she suspended her hand over first one switch and then the other. One would take the Gant to Earth. The other would lose them somewhere in the central galaxy.

At J-minus ten seconds and counting she let her lips form the words.

'Nine – eight – seven – six – five – (Oh! God!) – four – three – two – one!'

Her hand hesitated, then moved resolutely to press a switch.